FIVE
TUESDAYS
IN WINTER

Also by Lily King

The Pleasing Hour

The English Teacher

Father of the Rain

Euphoria

Writers & Lovers

FIVE TUESDAYS IN WINTER

STORIES

LILY KING

Grove Press
New York

FIRST EDITION

Published simultaneously in Canada
Printed in the United States of America

"You Don't Bring Me Flowers," words by Neil Diamond, Marilyn
Bergman and Alan Bergman; music by Neil Diamond; copyright © 1977.
Stonebridge-Music, Inc. and Spirit Catalog Holdings, S.A.R.L. Copyright
Renewed. All Rights for Stonebridge-Music, Inc. administered by Universal
Tunes. All rights for Spirit Catalog Holdings, S.A.R.L. controlled and
administered by Spirit Two Music, Inc. All Rights Reserved. Used by
permission. Reprinted by permission of Hal Leonard LLC.

These stories appeared in slightly altered form in the following magazines:
"South" and "Five Tuesdays in Winter" in *Ploughshares,* "When in the
Dordogne" in *One Story,* "The Man at the Door" in the *Harvard Review,* and
"Timeline" in *O Magazine.*

First Grove Atlantic hardcover edition: November 2021

Library of Congress Cataloging-in-Publication data available for this title.

ISBN 978-0-8021-5876-5
eISBN 978-0-8021-5877-2

Grove Press
an imprint of Grove Atlantic
154 West 14th Street
New York, NY 10011

Distributed by Publishers Group West

groveatlantic.com

21 22 23 24   10 9 8 7 6 5 4 3 2 1

For my brother Apple, with all my love

CONTENTS

CREATURE

The summer I was fourteen, a few months after my mother had moved us out of my father's house, I was offered a job on Widows' Point babysitting this old lady's grandchildren who had come to visit for two weeks. Mrs. Pike got her dresses fitted at my mother's shop and the two of them made these arrangements without consulting me. It wasn't like my other babysitting jobs, a few hours at a time. I had to live there. I can't remember the conversation with my mother, if I'd wanted to go or if I'd put up a fight. I fought her on so many things back then.

The Point was a frying pan–shaped spit of land that thrust out into the Atlantic. Beyond it, at low tide, you could see a crescent of rocks offshore, but at high tide the water hid them entirely. No doubt it was those rocks, several hundred years earlier, that made the widows who'd given the Point its name. My father still owned the house I'd grown up in, on the handle of the pan, and to get to the Pikes' from our apartment downtown I had to pass it on my bike. He was in rehab again, in New Hampshire this time, but still I kept my head low as I pedaled by. All I saw was the bed of flowers along the road, untended since last fall, new shoots and buds trying to push through brown husks. This was the third time we'd moved out and I hoped the last.

The road sloped down after that as it began its loop around the Point. An ornate sign announced PRIVATE WAY. High hedges hid most of these fancier houses from sight, giving everything an overgrown, Sleeping Beauty feel. As kids we'd ridden down here despite the warning, scaring ourselves into believing that we'd be put in jail if we got caught, but we never dared go down a driveway. Still, we knew all the pillars, all the plaques with the old names barely legible anymore.

The Pikes' driveway was much longer than I'd thought. There had been a hot sun on my back on the road but now it was cool and dim, huge trees shaking on either side of me. The only other person I had ever known to do such a thing as I was doing now was Maria from *The Sound of Music*. I couldn't remember the song about courage that she sang as she walked with her guitar from the abbey to the von Trapp mansion, so I sang "Sixteen Going on Seventeen" until a horn blasted behind me and I swerved off the road and down a shallow gully and tumbled softly off my bike onto last year's leaves.

Above me, a man in a black suit and a bow tie called down. "You breathin'?" is what I believe he said. He had an accent. He formed the *r* with his tongue, not his lower lip.

I told him I was. He did not step down into the gulch of leaves to help me, but he waited until my bike and I were back on the driveway. He had a long face and a perfectly round bald head so that the two together looked like a scoop of ice cream on a cone.

"You come to subdue the kiddies?"

"Yes," I said uncertainly.

"I'll meet you below then. Come round the back. To the left. Not the garage side." He made *ga*rage rhyme with carriage, the stress on the wrong syllable.

It was only after he had driven off that I noticed the car, its tinny engine and lack of roof and long thin nose of a hood. It was an antique. I heard the horn again, very loud, even at this distance. And nothing like a regular car horn. More like the signal at halftime of a football game. No wonder it had blown me off the road. The word "claxon" came to mind and floated there as I wound down the rest of the driveway. I was halfway through *Jane Eyre* for summer reading. I figured the word had come from that.

The house came into view. Slowly. The road bent and I saw a section of it then more as I went along until the whole thing was splayed out in front of me. It was a mansion. Gray and white stone with turrets and balconies and other things that jutted or arched or recessed that I had no words for. We'd always guessed it was a mansion because people spoke of it that way, but really all we could picture was a house like our small capes, only much wider and taller. But mansions, I realized, were not made of wood. They were made of rock. There was a great curved procession of steps up to the front door but I remembered about going *round the back.*

The back seemed to me no less fancy than the front, fewer stairs to reach the door but the same carved columns and stone balustrade around a wide veranda. The man from the road was waiting for me, along with a woman in a striped dress and white shoes. They led me up and into the house, through a dark hallway to a pantry with a square table covered in checked oilcloth and three mismatched chairs.

The woman asked me if I was hungry, and though I said I wasn't, she brought out saltines and slices of orange cheese. She pressed a small wheel with spokes into an apple and produced eight even wedges and threw away the core. The two of them sat down with me. I wondered why, if they had this whole house, we were in such a small, dreary room.

"Where are your children?" I asked the woman. I figured she was more my direct boss than the father.

I'd never seen a grown-up blush before. Hers was instant, the way mine was, and the worst shade imaginable, as if the blood itself were just about to spill out. "I don't have any," she said. Sweat glinted above her lip and she stood quickly to bring my plate to the sink.

The man laughed. "The children you're to be taking care of don't belong to either of us! Show her upstairs and straighten the poor girl out."

I followed the woman up three flights of back stairs, uncarpeted wooden steps with a greasy banister and a potato chip smell. We turned out onto a wide corridor full of light from long high windows that framed the blue sky above us. We passed at least five bedrooms until she pointed to one on the left, as if she were just now choosing it for me. But when I peeked in I saw a set of towels at the foot of the bed and my mother's green suitcase on a wooden rack. It felt for a moment as if I would find my mother, too, in the room when I stepped in, but when I did it was empty. I'd forgotten she'd driven the suitcase over on Sunday. The woman told me her name was Margaret and that she would be downstairs in the kitchen whenever I needed her.

"The littles have gone to the beach with their mum but should be back for naptime. They'll come find you then, I'm sure." Her accent wasn't like the man's. Foreign, but different. I realized they might not be married at all.

When she'd gone, I shut the door and looked around my room. It was the first room I'd ever had that had nothing to do with my parents, their tastes, or their rules. I felt

like Marlo Thomas on *That Girl*, a girl with her own apartment. It was a chaste room, with two twin beds covered in
the same white knitted bedspreads, their fluted oak posts
rising to eye level and tapering to pinecones. The bedside
table between them was small, covered with a piece of
calico, and had just enough space for a glass lamp with
a pull chain and an ashtray, also glass, with a bull in the
center and four notches along the edge for cigarettes. I'd
smoked a bit when I was younger, with my friend Gina in
the woods, but I'd grown out of it. Even though the ashtray was clean, I could smell old ash and I slid it into the
rickety drawer below.

I had a window seat! I rushed over to it as if it might
disappear and stretched out on my stomach on the long,
curved cushion. There were three huge windows that bent
to form a half circle—this whole half of my room was
curved—and it was only then that I realized I was *inside*
one of the turrets I'd seen from the road.

I pressed my nose to the old glass and breathed in its
dusty metallic smell and looked down at the gravel driveway and the shaved lawn that gave way to an ungroomed
field of tall grasses and a few wildflowers and ended
abruptly with a drop to the ocean. I thought of my parents
and their fights over money, of my father living in what my
mother and I thought of as a big house now that we lived
in a one-bedroom apartment, which wasn't at all like *That*

Girl to me. Though maybe to my mother—who was still in her thirties and had a pretty smile and, as she often said, a lot of things going for her—it was. I wanted to show each of them my room in this mansion, but then again I didn't. I wanted it to be all mine.

The ground suddenly seemed a long way down and escape far away. I pushed out thoughts of Rapunzel, a story that had always scared me, and of Charles Manson, whom Gina's older brother had told us about that spring. I opened my suitcase and took out *Jane Eyre* and the new notebook I'd bought. But I didn't feel like reading or taking notes, so I started a letter to Gina. I told her about the bike ride to the Pikes'. I told her about going past my father's and seeing the neglected flower beds, *all the death and new life tangled together*, I wrote, and surprised myself and kept writing.

Over an hour later a navy blue station wagon came down the driveway and stopped in front of the *garage*. My windows were closed but I could see the little boy was crying when he got out of the car and the little girl was asleep as her mother pulled her out of the back and draped her on her shoulder. I supposed I should go down and help them unload the car of towels and beach toys or scoop up the sleeping girl and put her down on a bed somewhere, but I didn't. I wasn't in a hurry to become an employee. I stayed in my turret sprawled on my window seat until, a half hour later, there was a knock on my door and the job began for real.

It wasn't difficult, at least not before Hugh arrived. Margaret made all the meals and Thomas, the man with the ice-cream cone head, did all the serving and the washing up. A lady named Mrs. Bay came for the laundry, including the disgusting cloth diapers that Kay, the children's mother, insisted on using. When I met Kay the first day, she attached Elsie to one of my hands and Stevie to the other and said, "I've got to pee like a racehorse, Carol," and dashed off. She came right back and gave me a hug and thanked me for coming, as if we were old friends and I'd stopped by to visit. I was aware of the age difference between us—I was fourteen and she was twenty-nine—but to her, because she spent her days with a two- and a four-year-old, I must have seemed older than I was. Kay was different around her mother, stiff and nearly silent. Mrs. Pike told us each morning in the breakfast room how the day would unfold. Kay nodded at her mother's ideas—Mrs. Pike wanted her to see old friends, play tennis at the club, visit her old German tutor who had said she had so much promise—but as soon as her mother left the room to go to her desk after breakfast, Kay turned to me and hatched another plan.

We took the kids to several different beaches, a whaling museum, an aquarium, often stopping after lunch at an ice-cream parlor where we made our own sundaes. In the early afternoon I played with the kids in the pool while Kay read her book on a lounge chair in the grass, then I took them up and put them down for their naps. They never resisted the naps. After the morning activity and the hot sun and the swim, they were ready to crawl into their cool beds in the dim house and fall into a heavy sleep. While I read and sang to them, I imagined going to my room and sleeping, too, but when I got up to my third-floor turret I always had a new surge of energy. I continued the letter I'd started to Gina all about my life in the Pike mansion. I read *Jane Eyre*. I suddenly felt so much closer to Jane, now that I, too, lived in a huge house and had charge of two children. Soon my long letter took on the tone and vocabulary of Charlotte Brontë, which Gina mocked me mercilessly for later. But I was trying things out, life as *That Girl*, life as Jane Eyre, life as a writer alone in her own room, which eventually, after a lot of other things, is what I became.

When the children woke up from their naps, I played with them outside on the lawn until hunger made them cranky and we went and visited Margaret in the kitchen for a snack. Dinner wasn't served until eight, when I'd wrestle Elsie into her highchair (she much preferred a lap, especially at that hour) then retreat to the kitchen where I was given my dinner at the oilcloth table. Sometimes Thomas or Margaret would sit with me for a minute or two, but they were always popping up to plate and serve

9

a new course. Stevie and Elsie rarely made it to dessert. Kay often poked her head in the kitchen, signaling that I should evac them upstairs. Of course they put up a fight. Dessert had been held out to them as a reward for good behavior at dinner, but they had "fussed," as Mrs. Pike called it, and their departure in my arms from the dining room was loud and trailed behind me like the tail of a kite all the way up the wide front staircase, across the landing with the two sofas beneath the windows, and up to their rooms on the second floor.

This is how it went for the first six days. Then Hugh arrived. He pulled up in a scraped-up Malibu sedan. We were at breakfast, which I ate with the rest in the dining room to help manage the kids' morning energy. Margaret was the one to notice. We all went out to the loggia, as Mrs. Pike called it, a covered portico held up by a series of arches facing the driveway.

"But Thomas is supposed to get you at Logan this afternoon," Mrs. Pike called to him as she began making her way down all those steps.

Hugh leaned against the car. "Then I'll go back to the airport this afternoon and wait for him."

"Don't be silly." Mrs. Pike, in stockings and pumps, took each uneven step carefully.

"Look at him. He won't move an inch toward her," Kay said to me. Then, down to him, "Where's Molly Bloom?"

"Molly Bloom's got a new job."

"She's not *coming?*"

"Nope." He tugged a canvas duffel out of the back. "You get me all to yourselves."

When Mrs. Pike reached the gravel, he put out his arms and said, "Motherlode."

She lifted her heels off the ground to kiss him.

"Who's Molly Bloom?" I asked Kay as we waited for them to come up. I had Elsie in my arms and she had Stevie in hers. They were both squirming but we ignored them. Kay and I had already gotten to that point of not having to communicate about the kids, not having to point out how perilous those steep steps would be for them.

"Hugh's wife."

Hugh looked too young, too disheveled, to have a wife. He looked like a boy coming home from boarding school. He was lean and seemed to be still growing, his torn, unwashed pants an inch short, his arms waiting for more muscle. And he had wild teenage hair, frizzy and unable to lie down. He climbed the steps with his arm around his mother and they looked like a pair in a movie, the rich old lady befriending the hobo.

When he got to the top he wrapped his arms around his sister and Stevie and squeezed till they squealed.

He turned to me. His eyes were a pale, watery green. "An alien in our midst."

"This is Carol. She's my mother's helper."

"Hello, Cara." He ruffled Elsie's hair instead of shaking my hand.

"Car*ol*," Kay said.

But he didn't pay attention. He reached down and lifted Stevie high in the air and broke into song about someone begging a doctor for more pills.

Stevie shrieked his laughter.

The song continued in my head. The Stones. "Mother's Little Helper." It thrilled me that he hadn't spelled it out, that he'd been confident I would get it.

"Put him down or he'll wake the dead," Mrs. Pike said.

Hugh set him down on his feet with exaggerated alacrity, then pressed his mouth to Stevie's ear. "You'll wake the dead," he said in a slow growl. "And the dead are our only friends around here."

Stevie sunk his face in his mother's leg.

"Hughie, he's four, for pity's sake," Kay said.

"Pity's sake? Who are you, Mrs. Milkmore?" He turned to me. "You know Mrs. Milkmore?"

"Talk about waking the dead. Jesus," Kay said.

"You think she's dead?" Hugh raised himself up and thrust out his chest and spoke with his jaw slanted to one side and a wet frog in his throat. "For pity's sake, Kay, go change that skirt. Your school is not called the Ashing Nudist Colony!"

"Oh God, you sound just like her. She really said that, didn't she?"

Behind them, Mrs. Pike slipped away through the door. I saw the white of her shirt and the tan of her plaid skirt flicker in a window on the way to her writing desk. Hugh was looking off toward the pool and the ocean beyond it. "I'm having wedding flashbacks."

Kay watched her mother through a window. "Well, we chased her away in less than a minute. Might be a record."

"Easy come, easy go."

"The thing I remember the most," Kay said, turning back, "is that minister weeping."

"That's the thing everyone remembers. He stole the show. Where did she find him?"

"I think he's the summer church guy."

"No, it wasn't. That wasn't Reverend Carmichael."

"Reverend Carmichael? How on earth do you know these things? We never once went to that church. I never know if you're shitting—" She covered her mouth.

Hugh stretched open his glowing green eyes. The whites were full of bright-red threads. He bent his head in front of Stevie's. "Mommy said a bad word."

Stevie giggled uncomfortably.

"So, flashbacks in a good way?" Kay said.

He looked off again, nodded slowly. He had more to say but did not say it. He scratched one of his bony elbows.

Then he said, "It was magical. It was like a long dream."
He turned back. He looked at me. "Elsie is making you a
lovely runny poop bracelet."

Elsie's diaper was leaking onto my wrist. As I raced up
the wide dark stairs, I felt light, my chest full of something
new and exciting, a helium that lifted me from step to step
and made breathing difficult but somehow unnecessary.
The poop had soaked through the useless cloth diaper and
rubber cover and I had to change her whole outfit. I hurried back down to the front patio, but they were gone.

Hugh changed all our rhythms. The children waited for
him to wake up. I waited for him to come downstairs
before we left the house. Kay waited for the afternoon,
when he would join us at the pool and she could talk freely
without her mother around.

"She insists that the children eat with us," Kay said
to him that afternoon, "but a fucking hour after their bedtime. It's the only time she sees them all day and they are
at their absolute worst. She keeps calling them *sensitive*
and *fragile*. They're fucking exhausted, Ma." With Hugh,
Kay sounded like my father after a couple of drinks. She
sounded nothing like who she'd been before.

Hugh lay on his back on the cement, his feet and shins
bent into the water. He was tossing one of Stevie's stuffed
animals, a blue bear with a white star on its chest, high up
in the air and catching it. Stevie looked on nervously from

the shallow end where I was towing him around in a red ring. I was a long-finned pilot whale, he told me, guiding his boat to shore.

"I'm not sure we're going to have kids."

"What? Why?"

Hugh didn't answer.

"Raven doesn't want them?"

"Stevie," Hugh said, "this bear wants to get on the boat." His throw was short, and the bear landed facedown in the water. Stevie moaned that the blue bear didn't know how to swim and I got it out quickly, before the fabric could absorb much liquid. Kay was still waiting for an answer from her brother, but it never came.

Hugh had married Raven (I wasn't sure if that was really her name or a name he had given her, like he gave me Cara, but everyone in the family used it, except when Kay called her Molly Bloom, an allusion I wouldn't get until twelfth-grade English) in the garden the previous summer. Before he arrived no one had mentioned this, but now it came up all the time. After a while I noticed it was Mrs. Pike more than anyone else who brought it up. I got the sense that it was an expensive wedding and there were still some outstanding bills in town (there were stores to be avoided, particularly the liquor store, and trips had to be made to vendors farther away because of it). Money was tight for Mrs. Pike, though I heard Thomas say once that that was all in her mind and she made terrible trouble for herself because of it. But Mrs. Pike didn't seem to resent Hugh for the wedding. She just needed to confirm, several times a day, that it had been worth it. For her, remembering it and talking about it increased its value, or at least helped her get more and more of her money's worth, as if they were still using it, like an expensive appliance whose frequent use justifies the cost.

Within a few days, I knew so much about that one weekend I could nearly block it like a film: Hugh's friend Kip's long and inappropriate toast at the bridal dinner about Hugh's old girlfriend Thea; Raven's black dress (that did not match her hair—despite her name she was blond) that made "the aunties" (not sure whose) gasp; Stevie carrying the rings on Night Night, his special—and filthy— little sleeping pillow; the weepy minister; the family friend who at the end of the reception drove right off the seawall and was very, very lucky the tide was out.

Until Hugh arrived, Mrs. Pike had never come out to the pool with us. Now she came out after her "lie down" every afternoon. On the second day of his visit, Hugh and I were playing seals with Stevie and Elsie. The children floated in their plastic rings and water wings and we dunked underwater in tandem to tickle their feet and listen to them shriek.

"You bited me!" Elsie said after several rounds of this.

Hugh snapped his teeth together and she squealed.

Margaret came out the patio doors, down the four flights of stone slabs, and across the sunken garden to the pool gate where she said, "Your wife is on the phone for you, Hugh."

"Hugh, me sir?"

Margaret's face split into a grin. "Hugh, you sir." He rose up out of the pool in one sinewy motion. The water sluiced off his head and down his back. His green bathing suit clung to his bum and I could see its exact shape, two bony teardrops. He gave it a little wiggle then, as if he knew someone was watching. He jogged across the grass and by the time he reached the steps his ringlets had sprung back up.

"Well, you can't say he's not still utterly smitten," Mrs. Pike said.

"No, you cannot," Kay said.

Without Hugh there, they seemed barely acquaintances now. Kay was stiff in her chaise longue, her hands resting on a facedown hardcover in her lap, which I knew she wanted to get back to. But Mrs. Pike, in one of the smaller upright chairs under the umbrella, had no reading or distractions. And while she didn't make continual conversation, she made just enough to keep someone from picking up their novel. I was glad I was an employee in the pool, now a gentle blue-ringed octopus who gave rides to gentle children. Stevie wore earplugs because he was prone to ear infections.

(Hugh teased Stevie by mouthing words just so Stevie would shout: *I can't hear you I have my pugs in!*) Elsie pinched one out of his ear and Stevie let out a screech.

"Isn't it naptime?" Mrs. Pike asked. Usually when she asked this it was not, but this time it was.

I gathered up the towels and swim toys, the diaper bag and snack boxes and plastic cups.

Kay said, "I can take them up."

Mrs. Pike said, "Let Cara do it." She knew my name but she decided she liked Cara better. There had been a girl in her Sunday school class when she was little named Carol whom she hadn't liked. "It's what she's here for."

I'd dried us all off as best I could but we dripped a bit coming through the French doors and through the library, little drops that sank darkly into the blue-and-gold carpet. I sounded like I was hurrying them. I sounded like I was concerned for the rug and trying to find the most direct route to the stairs, but I was taking detours, guiding them through sitting rooms and studies and short hallways, listening hard for someone on the phone. I wanted to hear how he spoke to Raven. I knew how he spoke to his sister (blunt, sarcastic) and his mother (softer, upbeat, the edge slightly dulled, nearly but not quite solicitous), but how would he speak to his wife?

He wasn't in any of the rooms. I spotted a little closet with a door ajar and dark dribbles on the beige rug. It was empty except for a shelf and an old black dial phone, the only phone I ever saw in that whole house. But the receiver was on its cradle and Hugh was not in the room.

He was on the bottom step of the front staircase, his elbows on his knees, head bent forward and hanging limp below his sharp shoulder blades. He didn't look up until Stevie poked him in the ear. He didn't straighten up. He just turned his head toward us.

"Hey, you," Stevie said in an awkward imitation of his uncle.

"Hugh, me sir?" he said. He looked ill, greenish gray, though everything looked a bit that way in that dim house in the middle of the day.

"What're you doing?"

"Thinkin'. What're you doing?"

"I'm being put down for my nap."

Hugh gave him a slight smile. "That sounds nice. I'd like to be put down for a nap."

Stevie shook his head.

"No?"

Stevie kept shaking his head. He was already out of his conversational depth. And he was tired. But he was blocking my way up, with one hand on Hugh's leg and the other on the first newel post of the banister. I could tell without looking that Elsie had already fallen asleep. Her forehead lay hard and moist against my neck.

"Do you like coming here to this house?" Hugh asked him.

"Yeah," Stevie said, swaying, shifting his small weight from the knee to the post and back.

"I remember coming here to visit my grandmother."

"*Your* grandmother?"

"Grammy's mommy."

"Grammy's mommy," Stevie whispered, trying to fathom what that meant.

"She only wore black, huge long dresses down to her ankles. She was the last Victorian. And the only ghoul I ever met."

"What's that?"

"A ghoul? It's worse than a ghost."

"Oh." He wouldn't want to continue that conversation.

They looked at each other, Hugh breathing loudly through his nose, Stevie still swaying from knee to post. I could smell Hugh. I knew the scent by then. It was sharp and unclean, even after a swim, and I knew I wouldn't like it anywhere else but coming up from his long taut body. I breathed it in greedily.

I knew I should nudge Stevie up the stairs but I sensed Hugh didn't want to be alone. Something within him was crying out for something. Neither Stevie nor I knew what it was or what had happened, but we were compelled by it anyway.

"How's your dad?" Hugh said. For a few seconds I thought he knew about my dad and the drugs and all the rehab places, that my mother had told all that to Mrs. Pike and they all knew and laughed about it at dinner when I was in the pantry, and my body stung everywhere at once.

"Good," Stevie said. "Busy."

"He and your mom get along?"

"Yeah." There was a question in it.

"Sometimes parents fight. Like you fight with Elsie. They don't do that?"

Stevie shook his head.

"Your dad is kind to your mom?"

"Yup."

"And your mom is kind to your dad."

"Yup."

"Do you hear them talking? Not to you and your sister but to each other, about grown-up things?"

"Yup. A lot."

"And they talk in nice voices?"

"Uh-huh."

"When do you hear them talking?"

"Most times. Morning."

"You can hear them from your room?"

Stevie took a breath for a big thought. "I think they're watching TV but I go in and they're not, they're just lying there looking at the ceiling and laughing. They're weird, I guess."

"They're not weird. They're happy, Stevie. Will you promise me you'll remember that?"

"'Member what?"

"Your mom and dad laughing. Will you promise? Even when you're old as Grammy you'll remember?"

"Yup. Okay. Good night." He laughed. "I mean, not good night but good nappy night."

"You won't forget?"

"About what?"

"You've already forgotten!"

"No I didn't. I won't forget." He laughed again. He didn't move to go upstairs. "Laughing is weird. Why do we laugh?"

"Probably so we don't blubber like babies."

"Oh."

Stevie took a couple of steps up and I followed. Elsie shifted with the sudden movement but didn't wake up.

"Can we read the red car book?" Stevie asked me.

"Sure."

We got to the landing. The air was warmer up here. We turned and could see Hugh now, still on the bottom step. He grew smaller as we headed up the next flight.

I lowered Elsie to her crib slowly, gingerly, and she did not wake up. I read Stevie two books, then he crawled into his firmly bound bed (Margaret made the beds every morning, tight as sausages). He was asleep before I'd gotten to the chorus of "Here Comes the Sun."

Back out in the hall I stuck my head out over the upper railing. Hugh was still down there. He moved and I pulled back quickly.

Up in my room I continued my letter to Gina. It was over fifteen pages now, the longest thing I'd ever written. I liked to run my fingers over the words pressed into both sides of the pages with my blue ballpoint pen.

"Where's Hugh?" Mrs. Pike said as I was buckling Elsie into her highchair that night.

"Davy Stives is home," Kay said. "They went into town for dinner." Town, to the Pikes, wasn't downtown Ashing. It meant Boston, an hour away.

"I hope he told Margaret."

"I told her."

Mrs. Pike frowned as she spread her napkin across her dress. It seemed like she was looking for something else to complain about.

I retreated to the kitchen before her attention could alight on me.

It was nearly four in the morning when the Malibu crunched slowly into a spot below my window. I felt a familiar dread as he opened the car door and got out. But he wasn't drunk. I knew drunk. I was already an expert calibrator of drunk and high and coked out of one's mind. He cut a straight crisp line to the stairs and took them easily. He opened the door quietly and disappeared. The outside light went off.

He didn't come down for breakfast. Kay and I took the kids to Drake's Island on the ferry for the morning.

In the afternoon we were back by the pool.

"How long have you known she wasn't happy?" I heard Kay ask him.

Mrs. Pike was out playing bridge so there was no chance of her overhearing.

"*Happy*." He said it like it was a filthy word. "Is your husband *happy*? Every day? Some days? What is *happy*? What is being *happy* in a relationship? Are you happy? Such a stupid word. What the fuck is happy?"

"It's not that complicated. You either like living with someone or you don't. You either like the commitment part or you don't. Maybe you don't like the commitment part any more than she does, but she was the first one to say it out loud and now you are acting all indignant, but it's really what you want, too."

"Gesundheit, Herr Doktor. I don't think so."

"Well that's how it was with Thea, right?"

"Thea? We're not talking about *Thea*."

"I'm talking about patterns."

"My wife, with whom I made vows on that patch of grass right over there less than a year ago, wants out. That is not a pattern, Kay. That's my life fucking falling apart."

He walked off and slammed the gate behind him.

They thought I wasn't listening. They thought I was a scuba diver searching for treasure that Stevie had hidden at the bottom of the pool. It was a skill of mine, splitting myself in half, pretending to be childish and oblivious while sifting through adult exchanges with the focus and discrimination of a forensic detective.

I was eager to put the kids down and write to Gina about what I had heard. *Hugh's heart is in fragments. What coldhearted she-devil could cease to love such as he?*

But they'd had chocolate pudding at lunch and weren't sleepy. Stevie had a plastic record player and only one record, a 45 with "Feed the Birds" on one side and "It's a Small World" on the other. I wanted to play "Feed the Birds" to make them groggy, but they wanted "It's a Small World"—over and over. They danced to it, winding themselves up and flinging their clothing off until Elsie shimmied out of her diaper and flung it at the wall where it made a dark urine stain on the wallpaper with roses. I whisked her off to the bathroom where Kay had set up a changing table. Elsie had a bit of a rash and I wiped her crotch and bum white with Desitin. I liked the smell of Desitin. I sniffed my fingers. It brought on something from the earliest part of my childhood. I sucked in another long deep breath of it. I tried to remember a specific moment, a place, but it was only a feeling. A good feeling. A warm, safe feeling I no longer had.

I heard Stevie talking and then I heard Hugh and I hurried to pin on Elsie's fresh diaper, but by the time we came out of the bathroom I could hear his steps going down the back stairs.

"Who were you talking to?" I said.

"My uncle," Stevie said.

"What'd he say?"

"He said he was looking for something for me in the attic."

"The attic?"

He pointed up. I hardly thought of my floor, with all those beautiful bedrooms, as an attic. "But he didn't find it."

The three of us snuggled in Stevie's bed. Just as I opened *Life Cycle of the Green Sea Turtle* Stevie said, "Oh, he said that you are a excellent writer."

"Who?"

"You."

"Who said?"

He was giggling, thinking I was playing that game but I was not. He saw I wasn't joking and sobered up. "Hugh said," he said softly. "Uncle Hugh said."

I speed-read through the life of a green sea turtle. I agreed to let them nap together in Stevie's bed. I shut the door and ran to my room, as if I could prevent what had already happened.

I'd left my notebook on the window seat, closed, beneath my paperback of *Jane Eyre*. But now it was open, turned to a drawing of Hugh's long, thin figure alone in the field where he was married. I flipped through my notebook with his eyes, trying to gauge just how incriminating it all was. A drawing of his car from my window, a poem about him touching my leg on the stairway, which hadn't happened. And if there were any doubt at all, my most recent entries to my letter to Gina spelled it out with great drama, as if from the moors of England: *You cannot know these blistering feelings—you have not yet met your Rochester. But believe me, they are so powerful that now every novel, every line of poetry, makes perfect and vivid sense.* And: *Like everyone else in the family I am swept up in the tide of him, but he is good and kind and funny and that tide is where I want to hang suspended always.* And: *At the pool he lies on his back on the concrete with his arms spread like Christ on the cross and I want to ravish him.* I did not know exactly what ravish meant. I didn't think it could mean anything as boring as sex.

Nearly two hours later, Stevie called out for me. I hadn't moved from the window seat. My legs were stiff and barely held my weight as I crossed the room. I'd have to quit. I had another five days left, but I would have to leave. Hugh had probably already told his sister and mother. I couldn't bear the humiliation.

The kids were flushed from heavy sleep, their hair damp at the temples. I kept them entertained in their rooms for as long as I could, but eventually they wanted to go see Thomas and Margaret in the kitchen and eat the cubes of cheese she served them and play out on the grass. I imagined that everyone in the house knew by now, that Hugh had already had a good laugh with each of them, quoting from the notebook as my father would have if he'd ever found such a document. I expected him to give me a pleased, knowing glance that would harden if I didn't see the humor.

But he did not. He barely looked at me when I followed Stevie out onto the patio, Elsie on my hip.

The three Pikes were out there with their drinks, sitting on matching wrought iron chairs painted white to make them look more comfortable.

"Does she want to stay in Florida?" Kay said to her mother.

"Her stepchildren won't let her sell the house. They all own it together and they like going down there for vacations." Mrs. Pike pursed her lips on the rim of her cocktail.

"But they hate her."

"She moves out for those weeks."

"Why doesn't she sell them her share of the house?"

"They don't want that either. They want her to pay for the upkeep and the taxes."

"But if they all have equal shares—"

Mrs. Pike held up her hand. "I have the same conversation with her every week at bridge. They have got her wrapped around their little fingers. I think she likes it. I think it keeps her close to William."

"That's very astute of you," Kay said.

"You sound surprised."

It was the most I'd ever heard Kay talk to her mother. It was forced, but they were both giving it a lot of effort. They were each trying to hide from the other the fact that Hugh wasn't talking, wasn't mocking them or the people of their youth, that he was sitting in his wrought iron chair slack and wan, holding then releasing big breaths without realizing the racket he was making. Kay had advised him to absolutely not mention the situation with Raven to his mother, but Hugh might as well have had a T-shirt printed up. I relaxed a little, understanding that as usual the adults were not thinking about me, and the words in my notebook were meaningless to them.

The children were playing in the garden below the patio, chasing each other around the rosebushes.

"Cara, please, have some salmon." Mrs. Pike built me an hors d'oeuvre of a cracker, smoked salmon, chopped onions, and capers. I carried the little tower of it carefully to my mouth. It was delicious. So many sharp flavors at once.

Hugh watched. "The Education of Cara—what's your last name?"

My mouth was too full to answer.

"Hyeck," Mrs. Pike said. "And she hardly needs an education from us. She lives a half mile down the road."

"She does?"

"Where did you think she came from?"

"I don't know. She seems a little sophisticated for Ashing."

"You're not making any sense, Hugh."

"Big vocabulary." His expression did not change but his white-green eyes flashed at me, straight on, the pupils tiny because he was facing the sinking sun.

"I suppose she does," Mrs. Pike said, not at all agreeing.

"Would you make sure they don't fall in, Carol?" Kay said. The kids were edging toward the fountain at the end of the garden.

"Charlie just cleaned it, so it's fine if they want to dip their toes in," Mrs. Pike said.

I was relieved to be sent off. I soared across the grass with my arms out, flapping, tilting, and when the kids looked up they screeched at the great hawk angling at them.

Behind me, Hugh laughed. I scooped them each up in my talons and spun them toward the fountain. I lowered them gently near the edge of the basin and they stayed pressed against me, laughing, their tummies bouncing against me.

"Her parents recently—you know." Mrs. Pike never used the word "divorced." She always left it blank. She didn't realize how well her voice carried over the grass. It wasn't true, though. There had been no lawyers, no papers.

Hugh asked something and she said, "I have no idea." Sharply.

Kay snorted.

"When on Friday will Dan arrive?" Mrs. Pike asked Kay, to change the subject.

The fountain in the center of the little pool was a birdbath that produced a small orb of water that looked frozen in place. The only way you knew it was moving was from the dribbling off the sides. The oval basin was painted a pale turquoise, nearly the shade of Hugh's eyes.

I told the children they could put their feet in. I helped them take off their shoes and socks. The water was warmer here than in the big pool and soon feet were not enough.

Stevie pulled down his pants.

"Stephen Pike Martin!" Mrs. Pike called.

I pulled his pants back up.

"Can't they, Mom?"

"In the fountain? No."

"Take it all off, Stevie!"

"Hugh!"

"God, Mother," he said. "Let them be children, for pity's sake."

"You and your pity's sake. Oh, all right. Cara, let them go. No one's watching."

The side of the basin was steeper than it appeared and Stevie slid underwater as soon as he stepped in. I leapt in with my shoes still on and I scooped him up by his armpits. Water sluiced off his thin hair and he blinked madly and I waited for him to howl but he burst out laughing, which made Elsie scream for me to bring her in, too. I was already wet from the rescue, so I tossed off my shoes and put both kids on my lap and we slid down the little slope. Raised up like that they didn't go under, but their chins got close enough to make it feel dangerous and there was much yelling and splashing, their naked bodies rubbery under the water, gripping onto mine and howling in pleasure. We slid a few yards until my feet touched the base of the fountain and we stood up and waded up the slope to do it again.

"You're a polar bear," Stevie said. "And we're your little cubs sliding down an iceberg." We went down again and on the way back up he said, "You should be nudie, too." He tugged on my shirt.

"No, I can't be nudie," I said. We slid down many more times. I forgot about the Pikes, about Hugh and Raven and my notebook, until the light shifted and I saw Kay at the edge of the fountain, her face strange, stripped of all kindness.

"Okay, that's enough. Pass me the children and go put some dry clothes on, Carol."

When I walked past the seating area Hugh's head was bent and he was pinching the insides of his eyes with his thumb and index finger. He was laughing, not crying.

"Don't you say a *word*," his mother said to him.

Margaret was coming out with towels as I was going in. She gave me one and said something that I didn't understand until I'd gotten to the front stairs. "Cover yourself now" is what she'd said.

In front of the standing mirror in the corner of my room, I understood. My wet clothes, a pink tank top and white shorts, were transparent. I had been nudie, just like Stevie wanted. But the body in the mirror didn't entirely seem mine. The breasts were fuller, risen suddenly like an ad for biscuits. And through the shorts and underwear my crotch was a dark triangle. I recognized nothing about this body. It felt to me that the mirror itself, more like a looking glass, really, in its old-fashioned frame, had conjured it up, that I hadn't had this body before I'd moved into this room.

I went down to eat dinner in the pantry with Thomas and Margaret in the darkest, baggiest clothes I'd brought. I sat with my back to the dining room, so the Pikes didn't have to see me when Thomas pushed open the swinging door. Kay did not call for me that night to take the kids upstairs, even though I could hear them fussing throughout the meal.

I thought perhaps Mrs. Pike would send me home before breakfast, but the next morning she was particularly attentive and kind. She asked me how I'd slept and showed me how to use the little egg cutter to lop off the top of my soft-boiled egg. She proposed that she take me and the kids to the beach club for lunch, and Kay could have some time to herself. She could make an appointment for her at the hairdresser's if she liked.

But Kay said she wanted to take the kids to a place called David's Animal Farm, just over the New Hampshire border. I'd never heard of it before.

"Why on earth would you go all that way on such a beautiful day?" Mrs. Pike said.

"It sounds fun."

"I hired Cara so you could get a break."

"Thank you."

"I mean, so you can have some grown-up time."

"I know what you meant. But I *want* to be with my children on our vacation."

We ate our soft-boiled eggs in the silence that followed, everyone except Elsie who had Cheerios on her tray.

Hugh pushed through the swinging door and laughed at us.

"The egg cups!" We were eating from little figure eight–shaped porcelain cups that matched the plates, pink flowers, gold rims. "Ah, isn't it good to be alive in 1905?" He reached for the silver egg cutter and pretended to go after Stevie's nose.

I smelled him and remembered how I'd put myself to sleep the night before with a story about him taking me out into the woods where there was this old tennis court no one used anymore and him teaching me to play and afterward kissing me, a tender, delicate kiss, not the gross kind you saw on TV when it looked like the two people were trying to eat the same piece of candy, and remembering that story—even more than Hugh himself—gave me a nervous stomach and I couldn't take another bite of egg.

Hugh wanted to come with us to the animal farm. His mother told him he couldn't, that she needed him to move some furniture for her. He pressed her on what furniture and why couldn't Charlie do it and she wasn't prepared for the fight. She left the room abruptly.

He leaned over to me, his smell stronger now. "My mother thinks you are trying to bedevil me."

"Hugh, stop it," Kay said. "Jesus. Carol, that is *not* what my mother thinks." She was pouring more Cheerios for Elsie. "Bedevil," she said and held it in for about ten seconds then broke into a fit of laughter. Hugh joined her and for a while all you could hear was the little snaps of their throats.

David's Animal Farm wasn't a farm. It was more like an amusement park for animal lovers. You bought tokens for the dispensers of food, which were just bubble gum machines filled with pellets. The pellets tumbled into your hands and baby goats and sheep would come running over and you put your hand out flat and felt their big black lips delicately nibble them up. Hugh squatted next to one of the machines, put Stevie on one knee and Elsie on the other, and gave them a steady flow of pellets. Soon they were surrounded by goats. Hugh started putting the pellets in his ear and on his nose and the goats mauled his face with their rubbery lips and Stevie and Elsie giggled madly until someone in a David's T-shirt told him to stop. They also sold milk in baby bottles to feed the littlest goats. We got bottles for the kids and I sat on the ground with Elsie and we held the bottle together as a tiny black-and-white goat sucked the milk down.

Hugh tried to put his face where our goat was. "I want to be a baby goat. Feed me!"

But he was quiet on the way home. Kay tried to get him to talk but he would only answer with one or two words. I was in back with Stevie and Elsie who wanted to sing, and while we sang I heard Kay say, "You scare me when you get like this."

We went through town, past our apartment, then out on the neck toward the Point.

"Why did they put these sorry little shitholes right here?" Hugh said. "Nice road, crappy house. Sorry about that."

One of the shitholes up ahead was my father's. I saw a woman in a yellow shirt crouched down in one of his flower beds. My mother. I felt a strange whirring in my chest.

Go home! I wanted to scream out the window at her. *Let all his flowers die.* We'd been through this so many times, the dry-out places, the circle of chairs, the specked linoleum, all the apologies and tears that meant nothing.

Before the kids' naps, we all swam. The day had grown hot, hotter than it had been all week. Mrs. Pike joined us wearing a bathing suit. She had some blue knots in the veins, but her legs were strong, surprisingly muscular.

Hugh noticed this, too. "Those Richard Simmons classes have been paying off, Motherlode."

I grinned, but she had no idea what he was talking about.

He looked at me. We were in the shallow end. Stevie was swimming in his wings back and forth between us. He'd said it for me, I realized. I was swinging my arms along the surface of the water and he was imitating me. I understood that I had his full attention now. I wasn't quite sure what to do with it. I'd never had any boy's attention before as far as I knew.

"Carol, I just used the last of Elsie's diapers in the bag," Kay said. "Would you mind running up and getting a few more?"

"Sure." I lifted myself out of the pool.

"Now where is she off to?" I heard Mrs. Pike say from her chaise as I unlatched the gate.

"Who knows, Mother." He was speaking loudly to be sure I heard. "But she makes *perfect and vivid sense* to me."

I walked quickly across the grass. On the patio I dried off as best I could before I went in and up to the second-floor bathroom with the changing table and the big bag of diapers beneath it. I shut the door to pee. My bathing suit was still wet and I had a hard time peeling it down and a harder time pulling it back up when I was done. I flushed the toilet, grabbed two diapers, and pulled the door open. Hugh was there, his hands on either side of the door.

"Just making sure you got the diapers."

"Right here."

We looked at each other. He lifted a strap of my bathing suit off my shoulder then set it down again. "You were a little crooked there. In your rush."

"I should get these down there."

"You should." He stepped even closer, closer than I'd ever been to a boy before. "But let's just step in here. Just for a couple of minutes." He took my hand and led me back into the bathroom and shut the door and looped the hook on the door into its metal eye.

"Now. You," he said. The whole thing was like one of my stories at night. It was actually happening. "You are trouble. I, like my mother, think you are trying to seduce me." He came close to me again. "Are you?"

I didn't know how to respond.

But he wasn't listening for an answer. He reminded me of my dad, going in and out of focus like that. He breathed heavily. I smelled mayonnaise from the ham sandwiches Margaret had made us for lunch. He slid his finger under the strap again, this time hooking it and pulling it off my shoulder. He did not lean in to kiss me, which was how I thought these things were supposed to go. Up close his beard was sparse, too much space between reddish shafts.

He pushed me with his body against the changing table. One hand started kneading my right breast and the other went up into the suit from below. It was a tight fit. The suit was from last year. I felt his fingers wiggling around like they were looking for a dime in a small purse.

"I know you want this," he said in my ear, in a voice I didn't recognize. "I can give you this."

He started rubbing me hard both on the chest and down below. "You like me. I read all about it. *All* about it. And I can do this for you."

He kept rubbing. I knew what he was talking about. I hadn't done it to myself, but Gina had told me about it. I wanted to wait until I had a boyfriend so that the first time I felt it I would be with someone and not alone in my bedroom and it would be special. I also knew there were times when it was not special. But I didn't know that it could be not special with someone you liked. This was not special. This felt like Hugh was doing some kitchen chore inside my bathing suit.

Sweat had broken out all over his face. "I can give pleasure, not just receive it." His head was tilted toward the window, as if there were other people down on the grass he was talking to. "I do care about other people. Other people are real to me. Cara. You are real to me." One of his fingers inside my bathing suit was poking into me.

It hurt, really hurt. I reached for his hand but he kept rubbing and poking. "It hurts," I said.

He pressed his mouth to my ear. "It hurts at first and then it feels really, really good," he said.

But it was burning me. "This is so *stupid*," I said in a voice my mother hated. I'd been using it a lot lately. It was probably the reason she'd handed me over to Mrs. Pike. I was embarrassed by the sound of the voice. I tried to yank his hand out of my suit but he clamped me tighter against the table. His shoulder was pushing against my jaw. I shifted my mouth slightly and bit down hard.

He flinched back. "Jesus."

You become a creature I can't understand, my mother sometimes said to me.

He pulled away and looked at me then smiled and came for me again. But I had enough space now to put out my arms and shove him off of me. The weird thing was, Hugh's body fell so willingly. He fell backward over the lip of the tub and his head hit the tiled wall with a perfect clack, like the castanets in "It's a Small World." It worried me that he didn't open his eyes. I picked up the diapers and unlocked the door.

I knew I should tell Thomas or Mary or call 911 from the phone in the little room, but I walked outside toward the pool. I rehearsed not what I was going to say to Mrs. Pike or Kay but what I would write to Gina from jail, how I would explain it to her, the way he went down so easily, like a slinky you just have to nudge at the top of a staircase. I needed to remember to bring my notebook with me to jail.

"Well, the diapers must have been somewhere in California," Mrs. Pike said.

Kay had either dozed off or was pretending to, with Elsie in a deep sleep on her chest.

I was saying things in my head but nothing was coming out.

"Look, Cara, look! Look at me!" Stevie called from the pool. "I'm doing this all by my lone self!" He swam the whole width of the pool slowly, his arms and legs beneath him moving every which way, his head between the inflated wings on his arms, his mouth in a concentrated frown.

"Good job."

"What's wrong with your voice?"

"Nothing."

"I'll swim all the way to there"—he pointed to the deep end—"if you come with me. You can be my own pet wolf shark."

"A wolf shark? That sounds scary."

"They don't have to be."

It would be odd now if I said suddenly that I'd bitten Hugh and also he might be unconscious.

"Look!" Stevie lay on his back then flipped over onto his stomach, put his whole head underwater, then flipped over again onto his back. A week ago he was too scared to be the only one in the pool. Now he was doing tricks.

"Mrs. Pike," I began, my voice still strange. But behind her something caught my eye. Across the lawn and up at the very top of the mansion, nestled between the peaks of the two turrets, was a small widow's walk. Hugh was leaning against its railing, looking out to sea. He was still in his bathing suit, a square white bandage on his bare shoulder.

"Did you have something to say, Cara?"

"No. Just— Would you mind passing me the fins?"

She had to bend down to reach them.

"A wolf shark needs her fins," I said and slid them on.

At the edge of the pool I let out a howl and jumped. I could hear Stevie cheer me on just before I went under. I wasn't sure if wolf sharks actually existed. At four and a half, Stevie knew far more about the natural world than I did. But I hoped they existed. I hoped there was such a thing.

FIVE TUESDAYS
IN WINTER

Mitchell's daughter, who was twelve, accused him of loving his books but hating his customers. He didn't hate them. He just didn't like having to chat with them or lead them to very clearly marked sections—if they couldn't read signs, why were they buying books?—while they complained that nothing was arranged by title. He would have liked to have a bouncer at the door, a man with a rippled neck who would turn people away or quietly remove them when they revealed too much ignorance.

His daughter loved the customers. She sat behind the counter at the cash drawer every Saturday, writing up receipts in an illegible imitation of his own microscopic hand and chatting like an innkeeper. She was too tall and too sophisticated for a Maine preteen. She made him uneasy. She had recently learned the word "reticent" and used it on him constantly.

"Isn't he the most reticent person you've ever met?" she asked Kate, his only other employee.

"Maybe not the very most," Kate said, not looking up from her pricing.

"But he's—"

"That's enough, Paula," he said, then, feeling an unexpected pulse of blood to his cheeks, fled to the stockroom in back.

Mitchell had good ears, and just before he shut the door behind him, he heard Kate's gentle reprimand: "I think as a rule people don't like being spoken of in the third person."

He'd hired Kate three months ago. She'd recently moved to Portland from San Francisco for a man named Lincoln. They lived in a small apartment in Bayside. On their answering machine, Lincoln sounded high-strung and full of anticipation, as if he only ever expected good news after the beep. Despite her strong résumé, Kate had unexpected gaps in her knowledge of books. She had never read *The Leopard* or *The Go-Between*. She had never even heard of Machado de Assis. Once he overheard a customer ask how many lines were in a sestina, and she didn't know. She was a reader (she borrowed and returned as many as ten books a week) but not a speller. On the dupe sheet, she wrote J. Austin and F. Dostoyevski. At the end of the day, when she stapled the credit card receipts to the ticker tape totals, she didn't always align the edges evenly. She let the mechanical pencils run out of lead. She had thin, sometimes dry lips that she picked at when she was thinking deeply and that he would have liked to kiss.

Wanting to kiss Kate was like wanting a larger savings account for Paula's college education or one of those infallible computerized postal scales for mail orders. It was a persistent, irritating, useless desire. He had been on two dates since Paula's mother left. The first one, over five years ago now, had been a setup, a friend of a friend. They'd gone to an Italian restaurant for pasta puttanesca. She'd picked out all of her capers and left them on the lip of her bowl, explaining that she was allergic to shellfish. Then she'd wanted to talk about his wife's departure. The story—his college buddy Brad coming to visit from Australia and leaving two weeks later with a box of live lobsters and Mitchell's wife—seemed to arouse her. He couldn't bear to take her out again and lost the mutual friend as a result. Thankfully, others had left him alone.

He hadn't been devastated when his wife walked out. People vanished. It had been happening all his life. His mother died when he was six, his father nine years later. His best friend from childhood, Aaron, had found a lump on his back—Mitchell himself had spotted it first on the beach—and he was dead by Labor Day. Even his favorite customer, Mrs. White, had died within a few years of the shop's opening.

Mitchell stood at the stockroom's one window and watched three gulls flap restlessly above the harbor. Thick broken slabs of ice, the size of mattresses, had been pushed to the shore by the tide. Out farther, beyond the frozen crust, the open water shimmered a luminous summer blue. In these kinds of cold spells everything seemed confused. Even the gulls overhead seemed lost.

Later that afternoon, Paula said, "Kate speaks Spanish." Kate demurred from where she was shelving, but Paula overrode her. "She does. Did you know that, Dad?"

"Mm-hmm." He was going through a mildewed carton a student had just brought in. They were good books, without writing or highlighting on any page, but the bottom edge of nearly every one had a pen-and-ink drawing of a hairy testicle.

"That's my icon, in my frat," the student said. "It's a—"

"I know what it is." Mitchell was sharp, even for Mitchell.

Paula glowered. She was trying to train him to be more forgiving of his patrons. That was her campaign, ever since she'd grown tall, learned words like reticent, and found him flawed.

After the frat boy had gone, Paula said, "I was thinking. Kate could help with my Spanish conversation."

Kate approached the counter as if she were a customer. "I'm not a teacher. I just lived in Peru for a couple of years."

"Are you fluent?"

He could see from her face that it was a rigid question. "By the time I left I could say pretty much anything I wanted. But it's been six years now."

She would have been living in Peru when his wife left. He hoped, with an uncomfortable swell of feeling, that Kate had been happy there, that if his and Paula's life had been redirected, like the course of a river, she had been the recipient of those higher waters. Full of this fervent thought, he headed, for a reason he'd forgotten, to anthropology.

Paula found him there, staring blankly at the spines on the shelf. "She said she could come on Tuesday evenings. Can she?"

"If you think it will help."

"I've told you Mr. Gamero never lets us speak."

He did not say that she'd never mentioned this before.

To the store, Kate wore faded, untucked shirts and jeans slashed at the knee. He was often tempted to tease her, tell her that just because she sold used books she didn't have to wear used clothes, but he thought she might snap back with a crack about the pittance he paid her, so he refrained. To the first Spanish lesson, however, Kate walked up the path to his door in wool pants the color of cranberries. Tuesday was her day off. Perhaps she'd had a late lunch date downtown with Lincoln. Worse, she might have had a job interview. It was an easy thing to find out. She was the type who could not take a compliment. If he told her she looked nice, she'd give the reason instead of saying thank you. But he was the type who could not give a compliment, so he just said hello and let her in.

Paula came flying out of her bedroom and dragged Kate back down the hallway. The door clicked shut and he heard no Spanish, just peals of laughter for the next half hour.

He'd planned to do some paperwork before starting dinner, but when he sat down at his desk, he pulled out Kate's application instead: 2/14/68. Just as he'd remembered. She was well into her thirties, plenty old enough to be Paula's mother. So what was she doing in there, giggling like a seventh grader? Her birthday was coming up. On Valentine's Day, no less. Maybe she'd quit before then. She might expect a gift, or he might want to give her a little something and she'd take it the wrong way. Or Lincoln would.

They emerged from Paula's bedroom flushed and watery-eyed. He quickly slipped the application back in its file.

"Entonces, nos vemos el sábado, ¿no?" Kate said.

"¿Sábado? Sí."

They passed his desk without noticing him.

"Bueno. Hasta luego, Paula." She added an extra half syllable to his daughter's name.

"Adiós, Caterina."

They kissed on both cheeks, as if in Paris.

He waved from his chair, not wanting to break the flow with clunky English.

When she came to their house the next Tuesday, she wrote down on a slip of paper (a bank receipt, he saw later, that stated she had $57.37 in her account) from her coat pocket her new phone number. She said she was moving closer to the store.

"With Lincoln?" Paula asked, and Mitchell for once was grateful for her prying.

"No," Kate said, as if she might say more, then didn't.

"Why not? He has such perfect teeth."

Paula read the question on Mitchell's face and said, "She showed me pictures of him."

Long after she left, he got up from his reading to start supper and realized the slip of paper was still crushed in his hand.

The second and last date Mitchell had had after his wife left was with a woman who worked in the insurance office next to his store. Sometimes she'd come in when she got off work, and even though she talked too much and only looked at the oversized books with photos in any given section, he agreed to go to the movies with her when she'd asked him. They chose a comedy, but she kept whispering in his ear right before every joke, so that everyone in the audience was always laughing except them. He'd come out of the theater excruciatingly unsatisfied, far more unsatisfied than missing jokes should have left him. He felt abstracted and disjointed, and it occurred to him that the sensation was only a slight magnification of what he felt all the time. He couldn't wait to get back to his car in the store parking lot and drive away. But she was in an entirely different mood. She nearly twirled down the street, swayed not too subtly against him, and asked if he'd like to get a coffee. He said no, without excuse.

The next day while he was unpacking a shipment of remainders in the stock room, he heard her through the heating vent. She was on the phone with a friend. "No," she said. "It wasn't that bad. It was fun, actually . . . Yeah, he is, but I kind of like that . . ." Silence then a long cackle. "I do . . . All right, details. Let's see . . . The high point? Oh God. Let's see . . ." Mitchell left the box half-full and went back to the front of the store. That day he didn't stay till closing but instead left at quarter of five. He did this for a week straight until one evening when his former employee, the employee before Kate, had a dental procedure and he'd had to stay. The woman didn't come in. She never came in again. He saw her crossing the street once, and another time she was behind him at Westy's, the take-out place up the block, but they didn't speak. He couldn't say when he stopped seeing her altogether, when she must have left the insurance company, over a year ago, maybe two.

He listened to Kate's new message in the back office when she was out front at the register: "Hi. I'm not here. Say something funny and I'll get back to you." But her voice was not hopeful. It was the voice of someone stuck in Maine for no good reason. He hung up before the beep.

The only time he ever got any information about her was on Tuesdays and Saturdays. The rest of the week, without Paula, they worked together in the uninterrupted professionalism he'd established the first week of her employment. It was as if she never stood in his living room or giggled in Spanish with his daughter. He often hoped that Paula would bring up Kate's name in the evenings, let something slip about her he didn't know, but she never did. She spoke instead of teachers, friends, projects, a concert she wanted to go to. In history she was studying Watergate, and she wanted to know what he knew about it. His friend Aaron had been an intern in DC that summer of the hearings, the summer before Mitchell saw the hard node on his spine. He and Aaron had talked on the phone a lot, sometimes until two or three in the morning, passionate talk about the implications of impeachment and then, that hot August, the resignations. Paula waited for Mitchell's version of the events, but what he remembered most now about Watergate was the feeling of being nineteen in a one-room apartment and the sound—though it had been silent for so many years now—of Aaron's hyena laugh.

Finally, when he began to describe the break-in, Paula said she already knew all that, and when he said that it was the end of an era, the government's undeniable breach of faith with its people, she said her teacher explained that, too. So he told her about his one-room apartment and how Aaron's laugh nearly broke his eardrums, and she was inexplicably satisfied.

On the third Tuesday, as Kate was leaving, the phone rang. Paula ran to answer it. It was for her, of course, so Mitchell walked Kate to the door alone. She was dressed up again; she had put her coat on carefully so as not to wrinkle her soft ivory shirt. She had thin, straight hair that she'd probably complained about (as Paula had about hers) all her life but that was clean and shiny and soft looking. Again he wanted to say how nice she looked but instead said that he hoped she was keeping a careful record of her tutoring hours. She nodded that she was and told him he didn't have to keep reminding her. He was embarrassed. It was his default line; it came out of his mouth when he wanted to say other things to her.

He watched her walk to her car, which, during the lesson, had received a light coating of snow. He wondered if she'd brush off all the windows or just the front and back. She didn't do any of them. She just got into the car, put on the wipers, and, without looking sideways to see him standing unconcealed at the window, drove away.

"Kate has a date," Paula said, catching him in the act of watching her car disappear around the corner.

"Lincoln?" he asked hopefully, more comfortable with an old rival than a new one.

"They're over. With some guy she met at the store."

"My store?"

"She just said 'tienda,' but I think so."

"She told you this in Spanish?"

"That's why she's here, isn't it?"

"Sí," Mitchell ventured uneasily.

The next day he told Kate she'd have to start addressing postcards for the sale he had every April.

"I don't mind at all, but you do know it's only the first of February."

He remembered her approaching birthday and the dilemma about Valentine's and said, "There are over a thousand to send out, so we should get started on it."

He set her up in his office in the back and waited on the thin stream of customers himself.

"Call if you need help," she'd said before he shut her in.

"I will." But he knew even if there was a line ten deep he wouldn't call.

Around two, a young man in a dark-green parka came up to the counter. Mitchell knew he was going to ask for Kate, and when he did, he explained that she was busy at the moment. He was careful not to indicate in which direction she was so busy. Unperturbed, the man asked where the art section was, then slowly made his way toward it, lingering at the new-arrival bin, the poetry shelves, mythology, psychology, before arriving at art. If he pulled out a book, he replaced it exactly as it had been, flush with the other spines and the edge of its shelf, just as Mitchell liked them. But he had bad posture and snarls in his hair. He could see Kate looking at her watch as she came out of his office. He couldn't think of any way to keep her from coming forward. She looked down all the aisles until she found him.

"Hey," Mitchell heard her say.

"How're you doing?"

"A little disoriented." She flexed her hand, the one that had been addressing flyers for the past five hours. Her friend didn't ask why, and Mitchell was pleased that he shared this information with Kate alone. "Let's go," she said. Mitchell's spirits plummeted.

She hadn't mentioned leaving early. She had to stay until six. She came around the counter to get her coat and scarf. "I'm going to grab something at Westy's. Want anything?"

He'd forgotten all about lunch. "No," he said, even though he was suddenly starving. "Only mushroom soup."

It was a very small joke they had. Once, about four years ago, Westy's had served, for one day, the most delicious mushroom soup he'd ever tasted. They'd never offered it again, but he'd never stopped looking on the specials board for it every time he went in. Occasionally he put in a request, but the teenager at the register clearly had no say over soups.

The edges of Commercial Street were covered in a thick, lumpy layer of ice, and he watched them cross it slowly without touching. But they were talking a lot. Blue puffs came out of their mouths at the same time. They opened the door to Westy's and disappeared. They'd probably eat at one of the booths. He couldn't very well complain if once in the three months she'd been working there she ate her lunch out instead of bringing it back.

There was a couple in the far room whispering in fiction. He'd been pricing a stack of books he'd just bought from a composer, but now that Kate was gone he'd lost his concentration. He went down the aisle her friend had chosen and pulled out, one by one, the books he'd looked at. Each one was a decent book in a sea, he acknowledged with familiar shame, of mediocre books. He would have liked to have an intensely intellectual selection—no confessional poetry, no mass-market psychology, no coffee-table crap. But as it was, business was precarious. Most intellectuals were like the composer: selling, not buying. A few days ago, a woman had come in with swatches of fabric and asked him to find her books only in those colors. Last week a man had been looking for *War and Peace*, and when Mitchell explained that he was temporarily out of anything by Tolstoy, the man asked if he had it by anyone else. It was a terrible time for books.

"Hey, where are you?" She pulled on his sleeve. "I got it! Mushroom soup!" She held up two containers. She was smiling as wide as he'd ever seen. Her nose was red and dripping and beautiful. "It better be as good as you promised."

Hadn't she already eaten? Where was the guy in the green coat? How much did he owe her? Questions swarmed but stayed behind the tight knot in his throat.

There was always one stool behind the counter and another that he used to prop open the door in summer, which now stood by the coat rack nobody ever used. He'd once wanted the store to be a homey place, the sort of place where you come in and hang up your coat and stay awhile, but it never had been. He'd never given any customer the impression that he wanted them to stay awhile. Kate found this other stool and dragged it around back, so that the two stools were now side by side, with a cup of mushroom soup on the counter in front of each one.

She took a sip. Her eyes closed. "I would wait four years for this soup," she said.

He felt as if he would burst. He'd read about this feeling in novels, but he was sure he'd never experienced it. Meeting his wife had brought him pleasure, or a sort of relief, the mystery of whom to spend his life with solved—or so he'd thought. But he'd actually been fairly content before he met her, talking on the phone with Aaron, eating tuna in his little room, reading from the stacks of books borrowed from the store he now owned.

Mitchell wished his cup of soup would never end.

They took a long lunch. Customers, as always, were irritating and disruptive. They were worse in this kind of weather. There was a focus that went out of people's eyes. They often forgot what they were looking for and stalled motionless in the aisles. When an elderly woman finally made it out the door, Kate grunted, imitating the way he had responded to her gratitude for finding her a book.

"It was *Middlemarch*," he explained.

"Which is a great book."

"I know it's a great book." He was aware of how much like Paula he sounded when he whined. "But shouldn't she have read it by now? She's only a hundred and thirty-seven years old."

"She could be reading it for the hundred and thirty-seventh time. Or she could be giving it to her granddaughter. Or great-granddaughter." She seemed amused, entirely uninterested in changing him. He knew it was like that at first with anyone. He also knew it might mean that she didn't care about him at all.

He tried to think of what it really was that had bothered him about the old woman. For once in his life, thought turned instantly to speech before he could stop it. "I miss Mrs. White."

Kate looked up from her soup.

"An old woman who used to come in here."

"What was she like?"

Mitchell hadn't thought about the actual Mrs. White in a long time. When he thought about her now it was just a feeling, not a person, just a deep longing. He hadn't known her very well. "At ease," she used to say to him when she came in. She'd sit on the hard pink chair in science, reading Stephen Jay Gould. They'd shared a laugh once, when a girl a few years older than Paula moved swiftly through the store to the picture of Thomas Pynchon that hung on the back wall and burst into tears. It was the only picture of Pynchon available then, and not many people had ever seen even that, a reproduction of his high school yearbook photo, teeth like a donkey's. "The only person who should cry over that picture is his mother," Mrs. White had said.

Kate allowed him his silence. She didn't try to reframe the question or ask another. Mrs. White would have done the same thing. What was she like? *She was like you,* he realized, watching Kate scrape out the last sip of soup with a plastic spoon.

"She was like you," he said, incredulous.

The following day he couldn't bear her to be so far from him and told her, at the risk of her finding more dates, that she didn't have to spend more than an hour a day addressing flyers. He stayed at the counter with her, but they spoke very little. He pored through the boxes of books people lugged in from their cars, she took money from the customers, and in between they priced in silence. He wanted to ask her if she was planning to move back to San Francisco, or somewhere else, but every time he rehearsed it in his head, it sounded like a boss's question and not a friend's. Just before closing, a customer came up to the counter and asked if they were related. "You two have the exact same kind of eyes," he told them. He was drunk and the comment was preposterous. Kate had warm thick-lidded brown eyes, and his were a narrow, suspicious green. The man didn't have a coat and they watched him lurch away into the frozen air. They were careful not to look at each other's eyes. It was only yesterday, the day of the mushroom soup, but it was already far away.

Mitchell comforted himself with the thought of Saturday, the day after next, when Paula would be there with them. But that night she told him she had play practice in the morning—she'd been cast as Rooster in *Annie*—and that her friend Holly had invited her over afterward.

Once he recovered from that blow, he saw on his calendar that the fourteenth of February fell on a Tuesday, the fifth Tuesday of Spanish lessons.

Saturday then Tuesday came and went, without change. On Wednesday and on Friday it snowed. He woke up in the middle of the night thinking about snow clinging to the ends of Kate's hair and the slope of her back when she sat on the stool, then scolded himself until dawn. He tried to think of how to mention, offhand, to Paula that Kate's birthday was approaching. But, as usual, she was three steps ahead of him. "I completely forgot to tell you," she said at dinner. "I asked Kate to stay for dinner this Tuesday. It's her cumpleaños."

"Her birthday?" He feigned uncertainty.

"Have you been listening at the door, Dad?"

He wished he had the nerve.

"What should we get her?" Paula asked.

"How about a brooch?" he suggested.

"A brooch? What's that?"

"You know a sparkly"—he put his fingers on his chest—"pin thing."

"Oh my God. You are not serious."

"Then make her something."

"Like what?"

"I don't know. A drawing. A necklace. Or, what about doing what you used to do to the gravel?"

"Dad!"

Mitchell, remembering the hours Paula had spent with her rock polisher, lamented the loss of the driveway as a primary source of entertainment and gifts. He knew he'd have to drive Paula to the mall.

They saw Kate there that Sunday in the food court. She was eating a burrito, alone. Both he and Paula had the same irrational impulse to conceal themselves, for fear that she would guess their purpose, and shadow her through the shops in order to discover her preferences. After lunch, she went to the perfume counters in Macy's. A saleslady offered her some powder on a brush, but Kate shook her head and said something that made the woman laugh. Mitchell's chest contracted slightly at being denied the words. Then they watched her weave through the smaller stores with their red streamers and glittering hearts and loud reminders like *Sweetheart* and *Someone Special*.

"She seems sad," Paula said.

Mitchell was relieved she'd noticed. He thought it was just his own wishful thinking.

Kate didn't buy anything. They watched her leave the mall, scan the parking lot for her car, then head toward it. There was nothing outside—not above or below or in the trees beyond the mall—that wasn't some shade of gray.

The cold had eased and everything that had been solid was now a thick, filthy sludge.

"It's an awful time of year to have a birthday."

Paula agreed. They stood at the door Kate had walked through. She unlocked her car, lifted her long coat in behind her, shut the door, and sat for at least a minute before starting the engine. She'd been born in Swanton, Ohio. She'd had her appendix removed when she was nine. She didn't like cooked green peppers or people in costumes or anything by Henry James. She had a mole on her scalp, just where her part began. With only this handful of facts, he admitted to himself as Paula drew hearts in the clouds she breathed on the plate glass, he'd begun to truly care for her.

They bought her a brooch and went home.

His wife had left because, she claimed, he was locked shut. She said the most emotion he'd ever shown her had been during a heated debate about her use of a comma in a note she'd left him about grocery shopping.

There was no reason why anything would be different, why he would be able to make anyone happier now. He was the same person. He'd always been the same person. He marveled at how in books people looked back fondly to remembered selves as if they were lost acquaintances. But he'd never been anything but this one self. Perhaps it was because physically there'd been little change; he'd lost no hair, gained no weight, grown no beard. He'd read a great deal in the past twenty years but nothing that threatened his view of the world or his own minuscule place within it.

Still, on the fifth Tuesday, as Mitchell made dinner during the lesson, the lasagna noodles quivered in his hands as he placed them in the pan. Nervous as a schoolgirl. He wondered where that expression came from, for he had never seen Paula ever behave this way.

Nervous as a forty-two-year-old bookseller was how the saying should go.

Kate had arrived with a small heart-shaped box of chocolates, which he'd set on a table in the living room. He'd been so startled by the gift he hadn't taken in the rest of her, and now he couldn't picture her in Paula's room, sitting at the foot of the bed where they always sat (he'd often seen the indentation after she'd gone). Every now and then, as he went about preparing dinner, Mitchell glanced through the open doorway at the box of chocolates.

He was just putting the lasagna in the oven when Kate flew past.

"Where're you going?" he said, unable to conceal his horror as she flung her coat over her shoulders without bothering to fit her arms in the sleeves and reached for the door.

"I'll be right back." The door slammed shut and he heard her holler from the walkway: "She'll be fine."

He went to his daughter's room. The door was open but she wasn't in it. On her quilt on the bed was a dark-red stain and a few pale streaks. Her bathroom door was shut. He stood in silence before it.

"I'm okay, Dad." She sounded like she was hanging upside down.

"You sure?" He couldn't control the wobble in his voice.

"Kate's gone to get some stuff."

He actually already had "stuff" in his bathroom; he'd bought it for her years ago. "That's good," he said. Kate's choices would be better.

He felt pleased that he was not overreacting, that he knew right away what had happened and hadn't called an ambulance. And then he looked down and saw the blood up close. He was holding the quilt in his arms. He didn't remember taking it off the bed. It was a quilt his mother had made and he had slept beneath as a child. The stains and streaks seemed like warnings. Soon Paula would begin complaining that he didn't understand her, didn't appreciate her, didn't love her enough, when in fact he loved her so much his heart often felt shredded by it. But people always wanted words for all that roiled inside you.

"How do you feel?" he ventured.

"All right. Kinda weird."

"Your mother used to get terrible cramps," he said into the crack in the door. He waited for the clutch that came with talking about her, like someone had grabbed him by the chest hair. "She got headaches sometimes, too. She took extra iron. We probably still have some. They're green, in a white bottle." He waited, but the clutching feeling never came. "And she had a bullet birth when you were born, you know. Thirty-five minutes, I think. We barely made it to the hospital. Not that you want to be thinking of that right now." Sweat prickled his scalp. Shut up, he told himself. "One time she was wearing these white pants and—"

"Do you miss her, Dad?"

"No." He was astonished by the truth of it.

"I don't either anymore. I feel like I should miss her. All I really remember is her walking me to school and holding my hand and giving me big hugs at the door. But I always knew the minute she turned her back I was out of her mind completely. She wasn't like you. I knew you were thinking about me always."

She was revising now, creating new memories out of what she was left with, but his eyes stung anyway.

When Kate came back from the pharmacy, he retreated to the kitchen. He could hear her coaching Paula, first in the bathroom and then through the door. At times her voice was serious and precise; other times they were both laughing. After a long while, she came into the kitchen. She caught him standing there in the middle of the room, doing nothing. She touched the quilt in his arms. "If I run cold water on it now, it won't stain."

"I'll do it." He went down the narrow back hallway to the laundry room with the big basin, and she followed. He never expected her to follow.

He turned on the faucet. She held the quilt up and fed the stained parts to him slowly. They had to wash it bit by bit, wringing out one part before starting on another. He wished, as in a fairy tale, a magic spell had been placed on the cloth so it would never end, and they could spend the rest of their lives right here, washing and wringing.

"You may have to undo some stuff I told her while you were gone. I babbled on about iron supplements and pregnancy and probably scared the lights out of her."

"You babbled? I thought you were the most reticent man in the world."

"Every forty-two years or so I babble."

She still had her coat on. It must have started snowing again. Melted flakes glinted like stars all over her.

He heard the timer buzz, then the oven door squeak open.

They hung the quilt on the fishing line he'd strung up across the room years ago. When they were done he could do nothing but look at her. She looked carefully back. Paula called them to dinner but they made no move toward the kitchen.

"Why do you think," he asked her, "that man said we had the same eyes?"

"Maybe he saw something similar in them."

"Like what?"

"Fear." She looked away. He'd forgotten how disappointing these conversations could be.

"Desire," she added quietly.

Love, he thought. It would come out soon enough. Words and feelings were all churned up together inside him, finding each other like lost parts of an atom. He didn't try to push them apart or away. He let them float in the new fullness in his chest.

She brought her hand to his face. It wasn't the face other women had touched. The skin wasn't the same. His nerve endings had multiplied. He could feel each one of her fingers, their different sizes and temperatures. His stomach made a long slow twist in anticipation of all that his lips would feel.

He pulled her close, but Paula came around the corner then, and they jumped back. His daughter, however, was grinning. She took them each by the arm and led them to dinner. She'd lit a candle and poured apple juice into wineglasses. She'd put the heart of chocolates by his place. Lasagna sizzled in the center of the small table and Kate was smiling and Mitchell felt, if only for this moment in his kitchen, if only for this one winter evening, that he might not need a never-ending spell after all.

WHEN IN THE
DORDOGNE

The summer of 1986, the summer before I entered high school, my parents went to the Dordogne for eight weeks. My father had been sick, and it was thought that France, where he had studied as a young man, would enable his recovery. Through the university's employment office, my mother hired two sophomores to house-sit for the time they would be out of the country. As I came with the house, these two college boys were obliged to take care of me, too.

We lived at the end of a short street in a quiet neighborhood. Our house was big and gray, exceptionally large for three people, though I didn't realize that until Ed and Grant arrived in a maroon Pontiac that first afternoon. The two boys stood responsibly beside me as we waved my parents off. Grant might have murmured something consoling as they disappeared around the corner, about how they'd be back before I knew it. And then, after a respectful pause, they let loose.

Ed ran into the house and circled the rooms like a dog just let off its leash, climbed up the front staircase and came down the tight back stairs and then went back up the front set again, whooping and whooping again, all the way to the third-floor balcony where he called down to Grant and me still standing in the front hall. Just as we looked up, he released a pale-green globule that landed right on Grant's cheek. Grant barely flinched, wiped it off with the bottom of his T-shirt, and tore up the stairs. I could hear them on one floor and then another, down across the back hallway to my father's study—I didn't tell them not to go in, though I was screaming it in my head—and around to my sisters' old rooms, my brother's old room, all of them having left before I could remember them ever having lived there, their rooms still stuck in the seventies: the girls' closet doors covered with McGovern-Muskie bumper stickers, my brother's with Nixon-Agnew and Ford-Rockefeller. I stood there frozen in the downstairs hallway, not with fear but with amazement, with revelation. I had only seen people behave one way in this house, prudently, laconically, in codes I could not understand but had learned to imitate. And now here was another way.

I was the martini baby, conceived, I'm sure, after one too many in late July of 1971. My parents already had their family: two girls in boarding school, a boy about to enter the seventh grade. My father was fifty-one, my mother forty-seven. It must have seemed slightly obscene back then, a woman of her age getting pregnant. I was such a deep inconvenience to them. That much was clear already, although not something I could have put in words. It was purely visceral, a confused shame lodged inside my gut, a sense that I had been terribly, terribly bad but not being able to recall what I'd done wrong.

My mother had walked Ed and Grant through the house during their interview, showing them the circuit breakers and the hot-water heater and the fire extinguishers. She took them out to the pool house and explained about the toilet latch, told them a man named Chuck would come by every Wednesday to clean and chlorinate the pool. She brought them back in the house and gave them each a glass of iced tea with a sprig of fresh mint, which grew beside the back door stoop, and asked them if they had any questions.

It was Grant who asked about me. "Could you give us the rundown on your son?" I don't think he knew my name yet. "When he should be in bed, what he likes to eat, where he's allowed to go on his bike."

"Oh, he takes care of himself quite well, really." She gave me a small smile. "The club's schedule is right there on the fridge if there's any question of where he should be."

They were just two boys, young men, I suppose. Nothing particularly special about either of them. Ed came from New England, a small town in northern Maine, and Grant from Pennsylvania. Ed spoke little about his family except in tight, funny vignettes, like his father buying his mother-in-law a cow for Christmas because whenever she came over to the house she complained the milk was off. But Grant told me long stories about his sisters' love affairs, his mother's battle with polio, his father's ashes scattered in their garden and how scared he'd been as a boy to touch the flowers that grew there.

That first night we had chicken noodle casserole and peas and crinkled french fries, all from the freezer in the basement.

"It's better than a supermarket down there," Grant said when he came up with an armful of boxes. They had carte blanche at the market—just had to sign their names—but Grant loved foraging down in the basement much more.

He made the dinner while Ed sat at the kitchen table drinking a Schlitz. But he didn't sit there morbidly like my father sometimes did in the evenings, forcing himself—or perhaps forced by my mother—to be present. Ed set his chair at an angle and put his feet up on another one and chatted. He was a great chatterer. Chatting wasn't something I was used to.

"How long you been out of school?" He had an accent I'd never heard before. "School" sounded like *scoal*. It sounded Scottish or something.

"Three weeks tomorrow." They had been boring, lonely weeks. I hated tennis lessons and trying to hit the tin can for a Coke when you served and sailing classes with all the instruction about winches and halyards and the folding and unfolding of the sails and never enough time on the water.

"Three *weeks*? My little sister just got out yesterday."

"Private school," Grant said over his shoulder.

"That right? You pay for longer vacations?" he said to Grant. And then to me: "You like scoal?"

"Not really."

"You like anything?"

I thought. I wanted to like something. I liked them, Ed and Grant, though I wasn't about to say that.

"Guess not," he said. "Trying to think what I liked when I was your age. How old are you? No, wait, let me guess." He pretended to tie a kerchief to his head then pressed his fingers on his temples. "You are fourteen years, four months, and one day."

I did the math. He was exactly right.

He started laughing as my eyes widened at him. "Your father keeps your passports in his top desk drawer."

His words struck me like a slap.

"So, let's see," Ed said. "At fourteen years, three months, and a day, I loved Celia Washburn. I loved her so much my jaw ached and—"

"You can't go in that study. *Ever*. You have to promise."

I felt Grant turning around behind me. Saw Ed glance at him. They were trying not to laugh at the weird possessed voice that had come out of me.

"Okay. It's a promise," Ed said. He shifted his legs and took a swig of beer. "So my mother took me to the doctor because of this jaw ache, and he said I had to stop clenching it so much and when did I clench it, and I said whenever I think about a certain girl and he and the nurse laughed. My mother was out in the waiting room. Then we got to talking about other things and I told him my mother wouldn't let me play baseball that year because my cousin had gotten clonked on the head in the outfield, the dolt. So when he called my mother in, he told her that I was a little stressed and that she should let me play baseball to unwind."

Grant was chuckling.

"Oh, the shiny knees and long ponytail of Celia Washburn," Ed said. "You enamored with anyone?"

I was, of course. Hopelessly. But I shook my head no.

Ed hooted. "Oh my God, you are a terrible liar! Le pire! Never mind. I'll get it out of you in due time, my pretty." He raised his beer to his lips, then put it down again. "So apart from her, who shall remain nameless for now, what do you think about? What, as Professor Marcus would say—remember this, Grant?—makes your heart sing?"

I felt so uneasy with all this interrogation, but I liked it, too. And yet I had no answer. Nothing made my heart sing. Even Becca Salinero didn't make my heart sing. She made it hurt.

"Nothing? Nothing makes your heart sing?" Ed swung his head to Grant at the stove. "What makes your heart sing?"

"Chicken noodle casserole. The full moon and the really thin moon. Sunday mornings if the *New York Times* isn't sold out. My nieces and nephews. My blue bicycle. Yeats. And Hermann Hesse sometimes."

"Hermann Hesse. Le pire!"

"*Narcissus and Goldmund*," Grant said.

"Oh, c'mon. If you have to read a German, read Mann, not that lightweight."

"Four hundred pages about a guy wrapped in a camel hair blanket? No thanks."

"What makes your heart sing, Ed?" I ventured.

"The venerable state of Maine."

"So why aren't you there now?"

"Oh, God," said Grant.

"It's Disneyland in the summer. Unrecognizable. Hollywood. Hate it."

"Well, that was impressively concise." Grant handed me the peas and said sotto voce and yet for Ed's benefit, "Sometimes *that* topic can go on into the night."

"Well, I didn't want to scare our boy here right out of the gate."

We ate. The food, though familiar, tasted better than when my mother made it. I listened to them talk about the part-time jobs they had just started. Grant worked the lunch shift at a diner out on the highway, and Ed paved people's driveways. Grant said he dreaded going to sleep because he was always dreaming about gravy, pouring it into people's coffee cups, serving it in shoes. Ed said his lungs would be paved by the end of the summer.

Grant had heated up a Sara Lee pie, blueberry. We gathered round it when he pulled it out. He started to cut into it and Ed said, "I know how you're going to do this, a miserly wedge at a time when you know for a fact we're going to eat the whole thing. Gimme that."

Ed took the knife from him and cut the pie into thirds and put a mound of ice cream on each of the enormous pieces. We ate on the porch. It was a warm, humid night and the hot pie and the cold ice cream were perfect together. Our lawn looked blue in the near dark. We could hear the sounds of a cocktail party down the street, the rumble of male conversation and a woman's laughing voice cutting through, saying, "No, no, don't tell them!"

"No, no, don't tell them," Ed said in falsetto. "Don't tell them, Harold, about our large animal fetish!"

Everything he said felt like the funniest thing I'd ever heard.

Ed finished his pie way before Grant or me. He set his plate on the porch boards next to him and put the fork carefully at four o'clock. "It's very civilized, being rich," he said. "Very mellow."

I'd always been told we were middle class. Rich was something else. Yachts and private jets. I remembered my parents and their plane flight. They would be over the ocean by now. I didn't know what a nervous breakdown was, though I knew that's what kept happening to my father.

From far off there was a splash. Then Ed started to laugh. "I heard that person dive into a pool and I thought, lucky bastard, and then I remembered *we* have a fucking pool." He lifted off his T-shirt. "Fancy a swim?"

I never swam in the pool at night. It was too scary to be the only one in there, my limbs white as an octopus. Even with Grant and Ed that first night I was a little scared, and embarrassed. They took off all their clothes but I couldn't. I changed into the suit that was hanging in the pool house. I thought they'd make fun of me for this but they didn't. They didn't say a word. I had never been naked in front of anyone since I was a baby and even then I wasn't sure. All my life my mother had been handing me things through a closed door, just her arm reaching in with a towel or soap or whatever I needed. One time when I was eight or nine I slipped getting out of the tub and she had to call my father to come get me. I remember how rough his wool jacket felt against my wet skin.

With the big underwater bulb on in the deep end, everything was lime green. Our splashes looked phosphorescent. I was aware of their bodies, fascinated by their bodies. Ed was smaller and more compact than Grant, with taut bulbs at the backs of his calves and a stomach with small bands of muscle. He had a thick head of hair but his chest was hairless, smooth as rubber. Grant was tall and lean but loose, strangely fleshy for a person who in clothes appeared so thin. Two small pools of skin hung at his narrow hips, as if used to drooping there above an elastic band. He had thin brown hair on his head, a sparse coating of it on his chest, and yet around his penis the hair was quite red.

Ed found me in the shallow end, staring at Grant hanging from the diving board. "Do you think he dyes it?"

"I heard that," Grant called to us.

"Well, do you?" Ed called back.

Grant dropped down into the water and skimmed the bottom toward us, his long legs doing all the work, his ass tight then loose, tight then loose, square and soft.

Grant crashed through the surface and took Ed in a half nelson and they struggled and threw each other down into the water and I swear I could hear my mother at the side of the pool saying, *No roughhousing in the pool you could drown each other.* Though when she ever said that I didn't know. Perhaps when my brother was a young boy and I was watching from her lap. I had a hard time thinking of my brother—Frank was his name—as my brother. He was thirteen years older than I was, more like a friend of my parents' who stopped in occasionally for a drink. It seemed to me he was always wearing a tie, even on Saturdays. He lived in the city and my mother lamented how little he came to visit, how much he worked. *He likes it,* my father often said. *Worse things than working too hard.* Frank rarely spoke to me directly, though I think he spoke a lot about me, for I was aware of a hum of talk, like crickets at night, that when I came closer receded and when I left the room resumed. I thought it was about me, though perhaps it was about something else.

At one point, Grant held Ed underwater for a long time, too long, I thought, and just as I opened my mouth to tell him so, Ed elbowed him hard in his soft stomach. Grant released him with a long whimper and Ed's head pushed up through the water screaming, "What the fuck?" and Grant seemed to be crying, though it was hard to tell with the weird green shadows and all the water already on his face.

Grant got out, wrapped a towel around his waist, and went inside to do the dishes. Ed swam laps back and forth. I was afraid their argument would be like the ones my parents had, a few sharp words followed by days of silence. But after Grant finished up in the kitchen, he came back outside with a beer and placed it at the edge of the pool. Ed glided toward it and drank it standing in the shallow end. He made a joke in French and Grant laughed and things were tranquil between them again.

Later we sat on the porch. Their clothes were back on and that was more comfortable for me, though still I was not entirely at ease around them and found myself shaking with nerves despite the heat. They drank beers and Ed suggested I have one but Grant said no.

"I cannot believe it's not Friday yet," Ed said.

"It's not even Tuesday yet."

"The smell of that stuff." He meant the liquid asphalt. "Le pire."

"Why do you always say 'le pire'?" I asked.

He gave a very French frown, a thinking, eyebrows-raised frown of consideration. He lifted his palms up to me. "When in the Dordogne."

I woke up in the middle of the night. Someone was coughing below my window. I looked down and saw Ed on the back porch rattling cookies out of a package. He ate five in a row then lit a cigarette. "Fuck," I heard him say. "Fuck that."

I went into my father's study. It was a big room, meant to be a bedroom. Bookcases lined the walls. They were crammed with books and papers and journals in no particular order. The cleaning lady had done that in the spring, taken everything that had been scattered around for years and shoved it on the shelves. His desk was in the far corner, a chair on either side, its surface clean and empty now. It was an old desk, with green leather inlaid on the top and fat brass handles on the drawers. I sat down and opened each one, checking for the gun that was no longer there. Then I turned around to the wall, stuck my finger in the hole between his diploma from the Sorbonne and an old painting of the sea.

I heard a cough in the hallway and then a tap at the door.

I spun around in the swivel chair, wiping the plaster off my finger.

"Can I come in?" Ed said, already in and coming toward me.

He sat in the chair on the other side of the desk. I tried to block his view, but he saw it anyway, the hole and the fissures in the plaster around it.

"Wasn't exactly a crack shot, was he?"

"I think maybe he took a bit of skin off his cheek. He wore a Band-Aid for a few days."

Ed smirked. He was wearing boxer shorts. It was a hot night and we were both stuck to the leather chairs.

"It's not here anymore," he said.

"What?"

"What happened."

"Then where is it?"

"It's gone. It's over. You can't find it, stroke it, coo over it. Time has stolen it away like it fucking steals everything. In rare instances, like yours, that can be a good thing."

During the interview my mother had asked Ed and Grant if they played either tennis or golf and they had lied and said they did, thinking that that was the kind of person she was looking for. In fact she had wanted to know solely for practical reasons, because if they did she would put their names down in the guest book at the club and they could come and go as they liked. That first weekend I took them to play tennis. On weekends you had to wear all whites and so they put on my father's clothes. It was only as we were walking there that I noticed Ed had forgotten to put on my father's white socks. I didn't say anything but Grant did, and Ed said he was going to move so fast on the court that no one would arrest him for his black socks.

I made sure we got court 8, the farthest one from the clubhouse. Ed picked up on it right away.

"You don't want to be seen with a couple of slouches, do you?"

He was right. I could tell by the swings they'd taken in the yard that neither of them had any form. I probably told myself I was protecting them from ridicule, but I was protecting myself. I could already hear my tennis teacher telling me how bad it was for my game to play people like that. Fortunately the court next to us was empty and the wild lobs they hit at first did not bother anyone else's game. I was disappointed by their lack of skill. After living with them for five days I had convinced myself they could do anything. They looked like buffoons, especially Ed in his black socks, who was clearly athletic and could reach everything, but once he got there he flung his body along with his racket at the ball with very little success. I didn't understand why they couldn't easily imitate my stroke, which I showed them again and again. After rallying for a while, Ed moved over to Grant's side and they challenged me to a set. I suggested a little more practice was in order but they insisted. I spun my racket, they called up, it was down, and I served.

I decided to crush them. I lifted that first toss and decided to shred them to pieces. I had never had that feeling on the tennis court before, the raw desire to win. I was a competent player, but I had more runner-up trophies than anything else. I determined that I would not let them win one point off me. Because suddenly I found I resented my awe of them, my infatuation with them both, and the dread that had already lodged itself in my chest of their leaving in the middle of August. I wanted somehow to even the scales a bit, to show them that I was worth something, too, that I had something to teach them, something for them to be in awe of.

My first serve was low and fast. Ed returned it with a punch, as if it were a volley, and I expected it to die in the net but it went over and I couldn't reach it in time. That was the only point, I coached myself, they were ever going to get off me.

I served to Grant. He spun around and whiffed it. Tossed a high one to Ed who backed up then rushed forward but reached it and knocked it over nicely, right to me. I smashed it back but Grant stuck his racket out, it came back at me, and I hit it crosscourt to Ed's alley, but he was there and gave me a lob, which I smacked at his toes and watched it sail far up as he scrambled back, not backward as I had been taught, with little steps, but sprinting to the back of the court and reaching it and slicing it at just the right angle to my back corner. I hadn't been ready to run and it flashed past me, ticking the tape. Ed let out a victorious bellow. I could feel the heads down the row of courts swivel toward us. We had all taken to grunts and groans and hollers. They got better and I got worse and I slowly relinquished all hopes of a shutout and just tried to scratch out a humble win.

In the end they beat me 6–4. I threw my racquet at the fence and stalked off. I knew what this looked like; it was the kind of behavior that was abhorrent to my parents. Any anger was dealt with swiftly and severely, quarantined immediately, allowed no audience. I expected Grant and Ed to react similarly, to urge me home that instant, remove me from this public place because people were watching. People on the clubhouse veranda, people walking to their cars, people on the courts, and even people on the putting green could hear me swearing and kicking tires in the parking lot. I was surprised by it myself, the anger that came pouring out all because a couple of hacks had beaten me at tennis. But they just sat on the little strip of grass beyond the court with the three racquets zipped back up in the cases and the balls back in the can. After a while I had nothing left in me and they came to where I was by a maple tree near the entrance to the club and we started walking home.

I was too ashamed to speak. They chatted away to each other, as if they weren't angry with me, as if they weren't embarrassed for me and humiliated by me. As if I were not, as my mother used to say as she whisked me up to my room, a little beast who needed to change back to a boy.

"Your family belong to a club like that?"

Grant laughed. "No."

"Look at that guy burrowing into those bushes. What do you think he's doing?"

"Look at the dog on the porch."

"He's waiting for him to fetch the ball!" Ed joked.

And when the man backed out of the bushes with the dog's filthy ball, they burst into hysterics. They thought everything in our neighborhood was funny.

"Layton with the sheep," Grant said.

Ed cracked up. "Sometimes I'm lying in bed and I think of that story and I can't stop laughing."

"I know. It might be the funniest thing I ever heard."

"What do you think he's up to right now? Do you think he made it to Alaska?"

"Yeah. Knowing him."

"With the girl?"

"That I don't know. I was never sure about that part of the story."

"Me neither."

After a pause, Ed said, "I hope he didn't take that girl. God, they only fuck you up so bad." Ed's face was red and he was staring hard at a stoplight ahead of us while Grant was staring at him just as intently. "Still fucking kills," Ed said.

I saw Grant's arm lift slightly then fall back down at his side.

Then Ed nudged me. I thought they'd forgotten all about me. "Ground Round for dinner tonight?"

"Sure," I said lightly, all the anger gone somehow.

We reached Elm Street, the main street of our town, with all its green canvas awnings and the store names written in white on their scalloped hems.

"Let's get a Snickers at Healey's," Ed said, and we turned down Elm instead of going straight on Winthrop to the house.

Becca Salinero and her little brother were choosing sodas from the cooler, their backs to us. I spun around and tried to leave but Ed grabbed me and whispered, "It's her, isn't it?"

I didn't answer but it didn't matter. He went directly to the cooler. I meant to leave the store but my legs were stuck in place.

"Don't worry," Grant said. "He's good at this."

"Good at *what*?"

"Good at making friends."

He waited for them to choose their drinks. Becca's little brother had taken off his shirt and stuffed the collar and sleeves down the back of his shorts so the rest of it flapped behind him. He was so skinny you could see every rib in 3D.

Ed pointed to the soda her brother had chosen and said, "What, no diet drink for you, Fatty?" And Becca laughed her deep laugh.

I hid in the back aisle while they talked. Becca and her brother paid and left.

Ed had found out that she was a counselor at the summer camp at the community center. When we got home, he said, we'd call up the center for the camp's hours. And then, he explained as we stepped back into the sun and the heat pouring up from the sidewalk cement, we'd make our plan of attack.

If I hadn't glimpsed her in the store, hadn't been physically reminded of her, I might have protested. But I was putty and he knew it.

"Interesting choice," Grant said, and they both cracked up.

It was true that Becca was going through an awkward stage. She had recently shot up, but only in the legs, so that, especially in shorts, her squat torso looked like it was supported by stilts. She had gotten her braces off in the spring, though now she wore some sort of thick retainer whose fake kitten-tongue pink made her real gums look gray and sickly.

"A diamond in the rough, perhaps," Ed said, forcing a straight face. "Seriously, it shows good taste. She's not hiding anything. She's like a clear stream. That's exactly what you want. I went for the other kind and it's ruined my life."

"Ruined your spring," Grant said.

"Ruined my spring, summer, winter. What did I miss? Fall. God, I can't even think about fall. Anyway, not quite as adorable as Celia Washburn maybe, a little *Animal Kingdom*." Ed stretched his neck and pretended to rip leaves off a tree. Grant snorted and Ed's voice quavered then righted itself as he finished: "But very sweet."

On the way home we passed the park. There was a pickup game out on the basketball court. Ed made a beeline for it. I cringed. When the ball went through the net, he stepped onto the court and talked to the tallest guy, pointing to me and Grant who had trailed behind.

"Get your asses over here," he said. "It's our ball."

Basketball wasn't my game. But after a frustrating set of tennis it felt good to hold a big ball in my hands. I had never played on this court. No one I knew had. It was for the public school kids. Between points, I looked around at my town: the gazebo, the swings and jungle gym, the baseball diamond, the stone library and its parking lot beyond. I'd never seen it from right here. I'd had my own swing set in the backyard, gone to the club for my summer sports. One kid on the court gave me a hard time, called me Richie Rich under his breath. But the others just played, slapped me on the back when I managed to do the right thing, were forgiving when I didn't.

Ed got them all laughing because he really couldn't do anything in this life without talking. He tried to derail the other team with his narration: "Okay, now Big Red's got the ball. Big Red's coming down. Does Big Red have boobs or pecs? We're not sure but boy are they distracting. They draw your eye away from the ball." He went on and on. Even as he was intercepting and fleeing in the other direction you could hear his voice trailing after him. Every now and then I'd remember we'd seen Becca and were going to call the community center when we got back and I'd get a fresh rush of energy.

Once we got her schedule, we arranged to run into her. Ed had an uncanny knack of being able to predict her movements so that each time, she appeared to be stumbling upon us and not vice versa. Ed did not let me hide in the aisles again. The first time was in the sub shop. We were already in line when she walked in. We had it all planned out. Grant, very naturally though completely scripted, asked me what time it was and I turned around to look at the clock on the back wall. I caught her spitting her retainer into her hand and shoving it into her shorts pocket.

She said hey and I said hey. Her hair was in a ponytail and she had on her light-blue camp T-shirt that was crusty with some kind of freshly dried paint or clay. She had the clearest eyes. I had no idea what the word was for the color they were. She asked me if I was having a good summer and I asked her the same. We told each other which books we'd chosen from the summer reading list. She promised me that *The Brothers Karamazov* got better sixty pages in. And then we placed our orders, which came quickly, wrapped up tight, and she left, saying she had to bring one back to the house for her brother.

"Only one sub for Fatty?" Ed said.

When she was gone he said, "She likes our boy."

"What's not to like?" Grant said.

The next time we saw her I was supposed to ask her out. But I chickened out. The time after that Ed did it for me.

"We're going to the movies tonight. Want to come?"

"Um, yeah."

"Um, yeah it is. We'll pick you up at six forty-five sharp."

"But you don't know where I live."

"You're in the blue book, right?" I said, as if I didn't know 67 Vine Road and the big beech tree out front and her mother's Volkswagen Rabbit (LL3783) and her father's Audi (KN9722) that sat in the garage they built last year.

"Oh, you're in the *blue blood* book, right?" Ed mocked afterward, exactly in my accent, which had never seemed an accent to me before then.

At first, of course, I feared Becca would fall for Ed. "Une femme qui rit est une femme au lit," he'd said once, and he was so much funnier than anyone I knew.

The third time she came out with us, we went miniature golfing and got through five holes before it started pouring and we went back to the house. Grant pulled out the big pot for popcorn and Ed went into the living room and flopped on the sofa. I said I needed to go upstairs and change my shirt, but I lingered on the stairs to see what she and Ed would do together alone.

"You're kind of a ringer at the mini links," he said. "You go there a lot?"

"My brother likes it."

"But you not so much."

"I just beat him so easily."

Ed laughed and said, "Have a seat." But Becca said she was going to go find me.

I made it to the top of the stairs before she saw me. She came up and we looked down over the railing into the empty hallway. It was warm on the second floor. We were damp from the rain and the heat felt good. For once my house felt cozy. I pretended to be looking all the way down but I was really looking at her sneakers and the little peds she had on with fuzzy balls sticking out the back. I looked up to tell her one was hanging on by a thread and she kissed me. Or maybe I kissed her, which is what she always said when we relived that moment afterward. I had always dreaded my first kiss, knew it was long overdue but had no idea how it would ever come about. I'd had intensely sexual dreams by then, but they never gave me any indication of how such things would begin, how I was to make even kissing happen. Although I had never said it in so many words to myself, I would have preferred to be a girl in those situations. But there was something about having Grant and Ed below—hearing their noises, the popcorn starting to bounce in the pan, Ed yelping to Grant about something—that gave me courage. You know what you're doing, the noises below seemed to be saying. We know you're up there with her and we're hoping for the best for you. I felt my tongue go into her mouth, felt her tongue hesitate then meet mine, felt she had no more experience than I did, felt her neck and her hair, felt for the first time that I was feeling what I should be feeling, as if for once all the sharp awkward fragments of my life suddenly fell into their proper slots.

The TV went on. Ed and Grant started laughing, which made us laugh. A navy blue light was coming through the small high windows in the hallways. I'm not sure I was ever so happy.

"You smell like a wet dog," she said.

"You smell like a wet mongoose." And we laughed and kissed, feeling like we were doing something dirty by talking while we were kissing, talking of wet things.

And then we went downstairs and ate popcorn and her cheeks were flushed and her lips bright red and it was raining hard now outside and I knew Ed and Grant knew everything, and everything—*everything*—made me happy.

* * *

I imagined—more than once, more than a few times that summer—my parents killed in a car crash in France. I imagined Grant and Ed moving in permanently; I wondered if my parents had a will and in whose care they'd planned to leave me. I imagined long courtroom scenes with my mother's brother or my father's aunt, both of whom seemed likely candidates for guardian, versus me and Ed and Grant. I imagined us winning the lawsuit, taking a big road trip like the ones we were always talking about: to Louisiana, to Acapulco.

To wish your parents ill, to wish that they would never return, seems heavy from an adult perspective but it sat lightly on me that summer. A frivolous, whimsical wish that I knew would never come true.

And it didn't. My parents returned on August 16 as they had said they would, at six in the evening as they had also predicted. My father seemed stronger, full of a loud bluster I remembered from years earlier. My mother hugged me several times, each time telling me, like a grandmother, how tall I'd gotten. And then she looked me directly in the eye—I saw it was true that I had grown; I had to look down at an even steeper angle to meet her eye—and told me she was so surprised by how terribly she had missed me. On the word "terribly," her lips crumpled out of their usual fixed position and she could not seem to right them. I held her gaze and said I was surprised by how little I missed her. And then we laughed. What else could we do?

"Let's get you boys settled up," said my father, and he led Ed and Grant up the stairs swiftly, without the torpor of the past few years. He opened the door to his study and I followed them in. From the bottom drawer of the desk he pulled out a three-ring binder that held his checks. He wrote slowly, one check for Ed, another for Grant. Behind him the hole was gone. I raked my eyes over the white surface until I detected a small, slightly darker area where it had been patched up and painted. I tried to catch Ed's eye, but my father was asking them which professors they'd had, to see if he knew any of them.

"How was the Dordogne?" Grant asked.

They were awkward and stiff, strangers in a house that was once their own.

My father slid the binder back inside his desk and shut the drawer. "The Dordogne was the Dordogne."

I knew it was a line Ed would savor, that it would become part of his lexicon with Grant. My father shook both their hands firmly and thanked them for taking good care of the house.

I walked with Ed and Grant down the porch steps, across the lawn to the Pontiac.

"We never drove to Mexico," Ed said.

"Or to New Orleans," Grant said.

"Maybe they'll go back to Europe next summer," I said.

"Start leaving brochures around the house." Ed spread out his palms, marquee-style. "Capri in July!"

Grant dropped his bag beside the car and hugged me hard.

"I love you."

It was as if his big arms had squeezed the words out of me. I was embarrassed and I was also surprised, because I'd always thought I'd loved Ed more.

"Aw, we don't like to leave our boy," Ed said and came in on the hug. I breathed in his smell of cigarettes and hot asphalt.

I think we all felt certain we would see each other again, that this was not a real goodbye. In a week, after they'd gone home to see their families, they'd be back in their dorm a few miles from this road. They had pointed it out to me from the car, a big high-rise in the midst of squat brick buildings, and I imagined our life together would resume there in a few weeks. I could see the beanbag chairs, the box of pizza, the newspaper spread out with the movie listings. But when the school year began, I could never summon the confidence to step on campus, let alone go into a dorm and up to the eighth floor. Becca urged me to at least call or drop them a line but the summer closed up and there seemed no way back in.

I can look back on that time now as if rereading a book I was too young for the first time around. I see now how in love Grant was with Ed, how Ed knew it and needed it even if he couldn't return it, how Ed was nursing a badly broken heart, and how well they understood what had gone on in my house before they arrived. I will carry that summer with me until I am, as Ed used to say, "passé composé." I have never seen either of them since, though I have read all three of Ed's novels and liked each one. I confess that I have hoped for some reference to that summer in them, a large gray house, a college town, a lonely boy whose parents have left the country, but there has been no sign of me yet, nor of Grant. It is strange to think that they both still walk this earth somewhere, that they have also had several decades more of life, that right now they are each lying down or standing up or reading a book or on an airplane or in a hospital room or a taxi or sitting in an office.

Becca, though, I married. I don't know how other people do it, not stay with the girl whose ankle socks made your stomach flip at age fourteen, whose wet hair smells like your past—the girl who was with you the very moment you were introduced to happiness.

NORTH SEA

O da's daughter refused to carry her own suitcase.
"You put too many of your own things in it,"
Hanne said.

Oda got out of the car. "I put in a beach towel for each
of us and snacks in case they don't sell anything on the
boat. That's all."

Hanne remained in her seat. She hadn't wanted to
come, and the sight of the sea as they came down the hill
into the village of Harlesiel had not moved her as Oda
hoped it would. It had not, in fact, moved Oda either. She
hadn't known she'd expected a lift, a change, until it didn't
happen. But Hanne was young, twelve and a half, and had
rarely seen the open sea like this.

Perhaps it was all the clouds racing to hide the sun,
great bright globs of them as if blown like glass from a

fat straw and shorn flat on the bottom by the wind. They muted the hard blue of the water. They stole the show.

Across the parking lot, a man in a green jumpsuit unhooked a long chain at the start of the ramp and signaled a truck to move forward.

"The ferry does too take cars," Hanne said. "Look."

"Just trucks. For construction and such. Get out now. People will be next and I don't have our tickets yet."

Hanne did not move. The man in the jumpsuit walked backward in front of the truck, flicking his hand left and right as the truck dipped down the ramp with a clank and onto the boat. It was a tight fit. The man patted the hood of the truck as one would a dog and came back up the ramp. He nodded at the pedestrians.

Oda opened the passenger door and pulled on her daughter's upper arm. It was so slight in her hand, a slender bone wrapped in skin. She felt how easily she could dislocate it from its shoulder socket. Hanne yanked free.

"All right," Oda said. "I will carry it from here to the terminal, but you must take it onto the boat yourself." She put the strap of her purse over her head so it crossed her chest, a style she did not like and associated with women twenty years younger than she was, and lifted the two suitcases. Neither was particularly heavy, but this short walk to the ticket shack required all her energy.

It was their first vacation together, just the two of them. Oda had been saving for it for nearly two years.

The woman in the ticket house, having assumed she'd have some peace until the three o'clock boat, was eating a mustard sandwich. "Better hurry," she said through a mouthful and slid the red tickets to Oda.

Oda left Hanne's suitcase outside the little house and showed the two tickets to the man in the jumpsuit. "One is for my daughter. She's on her way." Hanne was still in the car.

The man held up the chain that he would soon reattach to block the way down the ramp.

"Please." She wanted to tell him Hanne was in the bathroom, but the ticket shack was too small for a bathroom. "Her father's dead," Oda said.

The man lowered the hand with the chain. Its fat links clanked against each other. She was ashamed to meet the man's eye but she had to if she wanted her daughter to make the boat.

"That's hard."

A horn blew. A younger man up in a small window of the control room was pointing and exclaiming something you couldn't hear through the glass.

"You get on the boat now. Find a seat inside where she can't see you." He had a Low Saxon accent she could understand, but just barely. "She'll come when you do."

There were a few plastic seats, a bench, and a series of windows streaked with salt. She was the only passenger inside. Everyone else was either standing in the space in front of the truck or up the stairs on the small deck. Oda put her suitcase with the others by the door and sat on the bench.

The horn blew again, angrier. A metal crank hissed and thudded. She leapt up and looked out the doorway. The ramp was rising off the stern. A jolt, and the boat pulled away from land in a rush of white foam. Hanne's suitcase was still outside the ticket shack.

"Mutti! Look up!"

Her thin arms were waving with others on the deck above.

"Don't lean over so far," Oda said, but it wasn't what she meant.

A few miles out and the sky lowered and the sea rose and there seemed barely enough room for the ferry to squeeze through the two planes of solid gray. People on the upper deck got cold and came inside. But not Hanne.

When the island came into view, a dark slanted veil hung over it. Oda pressed her forehead against one of the windows. Nowhere else in this wide span of the North Sea was it raining.

She would make Hanne tell the person in the ticket house on the island (Oda pictured the woman eating a mustard sandwich, though she knew of course it would not be the same person) about the suitcase and arrange to have it brought over. She would make Hanne pay for it out of her small allowance. She would not be soft about it.

But when the boat slowed and she and Hanne stood in the pelting rain with the other passengers waiting for the boat to connect with shore, she could see there was no ticket shack here.

"I'll bring over your daughter's duffel on the late boat," the man in the jumpsuit said, as if she had asked him.

"It's not a duffel. It's a suitcase." She didn't want him to bring the wrong bag.

"And you tell me not to be rude," Hanne said and walked ahead of her up the ramp.

Over the phone she'd had the innkeeper describe in detail the one room he had left. A double bed, a green desk, blue walls, cotton rug, a view of the water from two of the three windows. And a floral armchair. What colors? she'd asked. He'd paused. Burgundy and pink. She was certain he was making it up. He'd already put the phone down twice to answer her previous questions. He'd tried to hide his disappointment when she said she'd take it for two weeks in July.

The room was precisely as he'd described it and nothing like Oda had imagined. He'd told her its dimensions and she'd measured it out in her living room as she spoke to him. But the actual walls made it seem much smaller.

"Everything all right?"

They were still standing in the doorway.

"There's only one bed," Hanne said.

The innkeeper looked at Oda. He'd explained on the phone that there wasn't room for an extra rollaway and she'd lied and said they were used to sleeping in the same bed. "It will be fine," she said.

He was also not how she'd imagined, younger, bearded, in tight padded shorts.

"Sorry. I've just been out for a ride." She must have been staring.

"On a horse?" Hanne said.

He laughed. "A bike."

"I saw a horse on the ferry," Hanne said in a tone Oda thought she reserved just for her.

He laughed again. "There was a horse on the ferry?"

"I saw it *from* the ferry."

Her tone didn't seem to bother him. "There's a stable on the east end. They rent out, if you're interested."

"I don't know how to ride."

"She'll teach you. Her name's Pilar. She's from Sevilla but her German is excellent."

"Pilar," Hanne said.

"I could give her a ring and arrange it."

"I'd like that."

Oda couldn't afford to rent a horse for an hour let alone pay for a series of riding lessons. Surely Hanne knew that. All her savings for the year would be eaten up by this holiday. She would have to slip downstairs before he made that call.

He left and they were alone. Oda snapped on both lights because the afternoon was so dark, but it only made things worse so she put them out again, and it was even darker than before.

It was true that the armchair was burgundy and pink. It was also true that two of the windows faced the sea. But the sea was indistinguishable from the sky, rain, and fog so what did it matter? Fritz would be laughing now, at the expense, the effort, the view of nothing. But she only felt guilty that she was looking out at wet blots and blurs of gray he would never see. He'd planned all their trips, always south, toward the sun. Now she understood why.

"You don't want me riding," Hanne said.

In one way she was lucky her daughter was only twelve and could only imagine that Oda was brooding about horses.

"I've always wanted to learn, you know."

Fritz had left her with debts on three credit cards, large debts that she had only just paid off this spring. She wasn't going to fall behind for something as frivolous as riding lessons.

When Oda went downstairs, the innkeeper was setting tables. He asked if they had everything they needed.

"Where is the nearest shop for crackers and such?" She did not want to tell him she would be buying the food for most of their meals and fixing them in her room. Perhaps tomorrow or the next day she might dare to ask for a small spot in his fridge for sliced meats and cheeses.

"Back down the hill, take a right, and it will be on your left. That place is expensive, though. If you like, I can add what you need when I place my order on the mainland. Delivery comes every other day on the morning boat."

"Thank you," she said, embarrassed. Kindnesses like that could strip her naked and she scrambled to cover herself up. "Perhaps another day. Today I'll just run out for a few things."

"Closed today. Sunday."

"I see."

"Shall I set your table for supper?"

"Yes, please."

She went back upstairs without having mentioned the horses.

Hanne had strewn the contents of Oda's suitcase all over the floor. "Why don't you have my shampoo?"

"Because you said you'd pack the little bottles we got in Genoa." We meant the three of them, a different we.

"And you brought that gross deodorant that makes you smell like rotten vegetables."

Above them light footsteps traveled the length of the ceiling, another heavier pair close behind. Silence. A wild howl.

"Great," Hanne said. "Children."

She went down the hall to shower and Oda sank into the pink-and-burgundy chair. She didn't want to be here, spending money on this room and its view of fog. She wanted to sleep in her own bed and go to work in the morning. Her friends, her sister, and the whole culture had pushed her into this vacation. She didn't want it. Hanne didn't want it. Why were they subjecting themselves to it?

She went to the window. It had cleared slightly. She could see the sea and it was not placid. The waves were churned up white and whipped by the wind. Far out, great fishing vessels vied for territory. The horizon line was broken by several oil rigs, jagged prehistoric creatures on strong legs. She felt the ferry's rumble before she saw it curve around the east side of the island and pull into the harbor. People were shimmering in their raincoats.

Hanne was back and combing out her hair.

"The ferry's nearly in."

"I can see it."

"Go get your bag then."

Hanne put down the comb.

She appeared below and ran down the street in bare feet with wet strings of hair rising up behind her.

The kind man met her with her suitcase. They spoke, a surprising number of back and forths that Oda could not fill in, and then Hanne came back up the hill, slower, with her bag.

* * *

They were Australians, the people above them. Their three long-haired children streaked around the dining room in their pajamas, grabbing decorations off the table and books off the shelves until the father caught up with them and they all disappeared in a flurry of giggles and flailing limbs.

"You were never like that," Oda said.

"You tamped me down early."

"Crushed your free spirit, did I?"

They ate in silence like the couple from Belgium beside them. The Australian man returned, the three children trailing soberly behind him.

"Do you remember the song you used to sing me about the girl in the polka-dot dress?"

For a time Hanne had begged for that song every night.

"Polky Polky I used to call it."

"Dot Dot, actually."

Hanne smiled. "Dot Dot. I thought you were the most beautiful singer in the whole world."

Oda felt pitched up onto the crest of a wave, like one of those boats far out at sea.

Back in their room there was nothing to do but get into bed. Cold air, much colder than it ever got in Munich in July, came through the lifted windows. The quilt on the bed was heavy, the sheets tucked in tight. Hanne took the right side, closest to the wall. The bed cracked and creaked when Oda got in. She shut off the light.

Here it was, the moment, the reason for the vacation, the one thing that had convinced her to spend this money. After Fritz died, Oda's friend Frauke told her that when she lost her husband the children had slept in her bed for a year. But Hanne, even that first night, wanted to sleep in her own bed. If Oda tried to cuddle with her in her room, Hanne said she was too hot and asked her to leave. But here they would be together in the dark, where perhaps it would be easier and safer to talk to each other.

"Are you comfy?" Oda asked.

"Mm-hmm."

"Sleepy?"

"Not really."

"We could tell each other stories."

"What do you mean?"

"I could tell you a story about something. About me or you when you were little, or Grandmother. Or Papi." She let that hang there a moment. "Then you could tell me one." Oda rolled onto her side to face Hanne. She hoped Hanne would turn toward her but she did not. She remained on her back, in profile, her face dark against the last blue light of the day.

"I'm tired."

* * *

Oda woke up several hours later. The room was black, the kind of dark that had terrified her as a child when she slept at her grandparents' in the country. It still made her uneasy. She turned sideways on the bed so she could see through the window. Out on the water there were specks of light from the oil rigs. Metal things clanged on boats moored in the harbor. Against their hulls the water sounded like dogs lapping, quick and frantic. She lifted her head off the pillow and found a few green lights closer in, running lights on the ferry in its hold. She didn't know it slept here at night. It made sense, in case of an emergency. It wasn't rumbling now, but she remembered what its rumbling felt like, and the thought of that comforted her.

When it was light enough she read in bed, turning the pages quietly, careful not to wake Hanne. Down below, plates were being placed on tables. The smell of fresh bread and sausage filled the room. Oda felt a racing in her body, an urgency that had no reason to exist now. She didn't have to get up for work or make Hanne's lunch or get her to her Saturday lessons or to church. She wondered how other people adjusted to vacations. It was such an unpleasant feeling, like gunning a car in neutral. It pulled her from the book she was reading. Her eyes could not take in the words. It was like the months after Fritz died all over again.

But he had been dead nearly two years. He'd gone to work at the hospital on his bike and been hit by another doctor in a car. The ambulance had traveled less than half a kilometer to reach him but he was already gone.

He'd died with less than two thousand euros in the bank. She'd been certain there was another account somewhere—he'd mentioned wanting to set one up after Hanne was born—with savings for her. He'd trained to be a doctor, but instead of going into practice as he'd planned, he'd taken a postdoc residency with a hematologist he admired, which led to another in infectious diseases and another researching the typhus outbreak of 1847. He'd had so much curiosity. There was always the promise of a solid regular salary just ahead, one more year, one last itch scratched. Oda hadn't minded, not really, not for a long time. She did the books for several of Fritz's medical school friends who had started their own practices and that brought in some extra money. It also made her feel safe, going over his friends' numbers. Fritz wasn't earning that kind of money, but he could be. At any moment he could have an income like that. Instead he died. And there was no other bank account.

Or a life insurance policy—another thing she couldn't quite believe. She sat in the office of the company where she had hers and asked the man to look again at his computer screen. She was sure they'd filled out the papers at the same time. Hadn't they had a joint policy? Sometimes names get dropped, she explained to him. It had happened with the same computer program he was using. One of her clients had it. Could she have a look? She expected the man to rebuff her, but he let her come around his desk, seize the mouse, and click away. She explained what she was doing, where she was searching. She never found a policy in Fritz's name, but a few days later she got a call from that insurance agent suggesting she apply for a full-time position that was opening up there. She was good at her job. She told people her story, the lack of a policy for her and her young daughter, and it moved them. It made them her customers.

Above her in the center of the ceiling a steady banging began, deliberate blows with a hard object against a bare floor. Footsteps. A voice that got louder—muffled words Oda could have understood had they been in German.

Hanne slept through the chaos, the banging, yelling, stomping. Finally they all went down for breakfast, clumping down the stairs for so long it sounded like a family of eighteen, not five. There wasn't exactly quiet after—they made a racket in the dining room—but Oda was able to return to her book. The racing feeling was fading, disappearing. The words started to make sense.

Hanne rolled onto her back, then over again on her stomach, a sure sign she was coming out of sleep.

"All your page turning woke me up," she said through her hair.

"It was the people upstairs. They were louder than a marching band for the past two hours."

"I didn't hear them. Just you. Can't you lift the book up so the pages don't drag against the sheet?"

"I do."

"You don't."

"We need to get up. I don't know when they stop serving."

"I'm not hungry."

"It comes with the room so you'll eat now." She never imagined she'd be using this tone on their vacation. "I'm going to take a shower," she said, before Hanne claimed it. "You can take one after we eat."

When she returned from the shower, Hanne was dressed. "You took so long. I'm starving."

At breakfast, Oda threw out some ideas for the day. They could go to the beach or walk into town or out on the breakwater to the red-and-white-striped lighthouse they saw from the ferry. They could go to the public pool or hike up the hill in the center of the island. Hanne made a face after every idea. Oda would have liked to ask the innkeeper what other sullen, ungrateful twelve-year-olds did on the island to amuse themselves, but she feared he'd mention the horseback riding. She worried that even without her asking this he would mention it, so she let him deliver their food and coffee without making any eye contact or saying anything but thank you.

Oda had a clear view of the Australians across the dining room. It was a struggle to get all three children to stay in their seats. None of them could have been older than six, yet none was a baby you could strap down. The parents looked like tired zookeepers, not angry, just overwhelmed by the physical demands. He was a tall, skinny man with a thick batch of blond ringlets and a nose that came to a sharp pencil point. His wife was probably his age, early thirties, but could have passed as a teenager in her sari and long unbrushed hair. She looked like the older girls Oda remembered from school, the girls her brother had liked but could not get, who never had rides home and whose eyes were pink and slitty from smoking pot and whose lips were always red and puffed up, like they'd been kissing all day. The Australians' children required so much of their attention that they were turned away from each other for most of the meal. But Oda caught one moment when he gave her a spoonful of something from a bowl, and he watched her reaction and smiled after she nodded that it was good.

"How are your eggs?" she asked Hanne.

"They're okay."

"Would you like to try mine?" She cut a corner of her waffle and added a strawberry to the fork.

Hanne looked horrified. "I know what waffles taste like." After a few more bites of egg she said, "You're being really weird, you know."

Oda asked for a second cup of coffee, then followed the innkeeper back into the kitchen, startling him when he turned back around with the coffee pot. "I'm wondering

111

if you have the name and number of the woman with the horses. For my daughter. For lessons."

That afternoon, Oda made tea in the kitchen and brought it up to the room. She turned the pink-and-burgundy chair around so that it faced the two windows that faced the sea and sat in it. The ferry came in. Oda watched it empty out— day-trippers with bicycles, repairmen in work outfits, islanders carrying crates of groceries—and fill up again. Her man was there. He guided the mail truck onto the boat then stood chatting with people boarding and with people who had no plans to board. There were many of these, folks milling about simply because the ferry was in, not because they were coming or going. The sky was still gray but not as low and compressive. Gulls skimmed the water then rose up so high their bodies evaporated into cloud. Up from the harbor came the sounds of men on boats talking over the engines and the rumble of the ferry as it pulled away from shore. The air through the windows came in gusts of hot and cold and after a while she could not smell the tang of the sea that had been so strong when she first sat down.

When Hanne came back, Oda had not yet sipped her tea or lifted her book from her lap.

"What happened?"

"What do you mean?"

"Why are you back so soon?" Oda looked at her watch. Three hours had gone by. "Oh," she said, confused.

"I rode a horse."

"You rode a horse?" Oda said but with too much surprise.

Hanne scowled. "That was the plan, wasn't it?" But she couldn't cover up all her pleasure. Oda could see it in the flushed streaks across her face.

"How was it?"

"It was okay."

She wasn't going to share any part of it. A few years ago she would have told Oda everything, wide-eyed and shrill, spinning around in what she and Fritz used to call her happy dance, unable to contain her joy. Adults hid their pain, their fears, their failure, but adolescents hid their happiness, as if to reveal it would risk its loss.

"Are you wearing my socks?" Hanne said.

"My feet were cold and these are so fuzzy and warm."

"Take them off. I was saving them."

Also, there was no correlation between happiness and kindness.

Hanne rode every afternoon that week. More than half a month's salary. Oda put it on a credit card she had only recently paid off. But those hours were Oda's respite as much as Hanne's, her vacation from her vacation. She didn't walk to the lighthouse Hanne refused to visit or go the maritime museum or have a beer in the lovely garden of the pub she heard the innkeeper tell guests about. She sat in her chair with her book and her tea and looked out the window. The sky rarely cleared and never for more than an hour or two. The ferry came in and out. Sometimes if she leaned all the way to the glass and looked far to the left at just the right moment she saw Hanne on the back of a horse on the long East Beach, hooves flashing through shallow water.

After a week, Hanne became more amenable to excursions in the morning. She even came back from the stables with ideas of places she'd like to go. They walked several kilometers to a place called the Burger Meister run by Americans. Instead of the whaling museum, Hanne showed her the graveyard of whalebones in the woods behind it. Every few weeks, Hanne told her, people from the museum removed the pile, but after a few days another stack of bones took its place. If their morning together went well, Oda would tell herself that tonight, *tonight* she would insist that they talk in the dark, that Hanne listen to one of the stories Fritz used to tell her about his childhood in Fürth or about their courtship or the strange trip they'd taken to Luxembourg before Hanne was born. She felt like a suitor, a seducer. She bought Hanne a bracelet and gave it to her at dinner. She encouraged her to have coffee or caffeinated tea with dessert. But no matter the good mood she might have lured her daughter into during the day, once in bed if Oda tried to start a conversation, Hanne shut it down. "Can't we just listen to the sea," she might say, or more violently: "I cannot listen to your voice anymore today."

At lunch one day, Oda tried to explain herself and the stories about Fritz she wanted Hanne to hear. "We don't talk about him enough. Or about his death. I don't want you to think I can't talk about it. I can. I will. I want to."

"Okay," Hanne said.

"So would you like to?"

"I don't know. Not right now."

"Tonight?"

"No."

"When?"

"I don't know. I don't know what you want me to say."

"I don't want you to say anything in particular. I just don't think the silence is healthy. I grew up with parents who never talked about the things that mattered, the things that pained them."

"The war?"

"Yes, the war was one of those things."

"So Papi's death is like the war and I'm like a Nazi who won't talk about it?"

"Hanne. You know what I'm saying. I don't want you to believe when you're older that you had a mother who didn't want to talk about things, because I do."

"Okay, if I promise never to say that you didn't talk about things can we stop having this conversation?"

"I met him in French class."

"Yeah, I know. He thought it was a history class but he didn't leave because he saw the back of your head."

Well, that was a bit of an exaggeration but she let it slide.

"I know the stories. I have a ton of photographs. I remember him."

"Do you miss him still?"

"I guess."

"Do you feel it was unfair that he died?"

"Of course. He only got half a life. Maybe less."

"But unfair to you."

"I guess so. But it's not like I knew him all that well."

"What do you mean?"

"He worked a lot."

"He was home for dinner nearly every night. He helped you with your homework."

"Once maybe."

"Hanne, no. Many nights."

"And on weekends he went to conferences."

"A few times a year. And sometimes we went with him. To Barcelona, remember?" She had a memory of the three of them in a park near their hotel, but she also had a memory of buying Hanne a doll made out of palm fronds, because Hanne had stayed home with Fritz's mother. Which was true? She wasn't sure.

"Is this talking? Because it feels like you're telling me what I should remember."

Three days before she and Hanne left the island, Oda had her first real conversation with the Australians.

She'd come downstairs without Hanne, who'd told her the night before she wanted to sleep in. Oda took her seat at the table they always sat at, then wished she'd chosen the other chair instead. Without Hanne in front of her she faced the Australians without obstruction.

"Guten Morgen," the husband said. He had a fine but exaggerated accent, too bouncy.

"How are you?" Oda said in English.

"Ah, as well as can be expected in the third week of vacation with these ankle biters."

She understood the gist, if not every word. The oldest child was pouring a packet of sugar into his hair. His father grabbed it out of his hand and swiped away the sugar on the boy's head. Some crystals pinged against Oda's plate. "Sorry," he said. "And you? How are you?"

Did he know? Of course he didn't. But for so long now when someone asked how she was they loaded it with pity and braced themselves for her reply, as if she had the power to hurt them with the truth.

"I'm fine," she said lightly, because for once she could. To him she was just a woman with her daughter, not a tragedy. "I sleep well by the sea." Or was it *at* the sea? She could never keep the British and American prepositions straight, and who knew what the Australians did.

"I do as well." He smiled at her, a charmer with his wild hair and flashing green eyes. And that long lean body. He reached over to take a slice of ham from his daughter's plate and his torso stretched the length of the table, the ribs of his back in relief through his thin T-shirt.

"Does your daughter babysit?" his wife asked, getting most of the ham back for the daughter who had begun to scream.

"No, she doesn't."

Imagine Hanne trying to control this brood.

Her own breakfast came then and she tucked in, keeping her eyes down. When they left, the husband said, "Cheers." His wife handed him the little girl. Oda wondered if one of them would die early and leave the other stunned for a time.

That evening, Hanne announced she was going to watch the Australian children the next day.

"Why did you tell them I don't babysit?"

"Because you never have. And because you can hear them up there. They're holy terrors. Plus, they don't speak German."

"I know English, Mother," Hanne said, in English.

Oda laughed.

"What? That's how you say it."

"Your voice. It's deeper in English."

Hanne nearly laughed, too. "It's because we've had Mr. Manfield for so many years and he can sing Osmin's aria, which goes down to D-2." When Oda didn't respond, she added, "The lowest solo note in all of opera."

Fritz's father paid for piano lessons for Hanne, though he hadn't visited since the funeral. He paid the music teacher directly by mail, as if Oda might try to skim off the top.

Hanne looked at her as if she should say something, but Oda was angry at Fritz's father now and went down the hall to the bathroom.

The Australian couple had hired a boat to take them to some deep-sea caves. Oda had read about them. They sounded terrifying. It was an hour out and an hour back and they'd probably spend another hour splashing around, the husband told Hanne at breakfast.

They looked at the clock together. "So we'll be back around eleven thirty, give or take a few," he said. "The critters are a bit wild in the streets. Best to just keep them upstairs where they have their toys and their books."

Oda chortled to herself. Those were not children who could sit down and listen to a book.

But she was wrong. Hanne took them up to the third floor and Oda, after waiting a few minutes, went quietly up the stairs and listened at the door.

"Which of this do you like?" Hanne said in her low English voice. "The ducks or . . . what one this called?"

"Ants!" one of the boys said.

"The ants? You choose the ants book?"

"No, the ducks," the little girl said. The boys didn't argue.

Hanne read to them about the ducks, then the ants. Then a story about a little boy in the city who collected animals on the roof without his parents knowing.

"I have a barn. Here. With lots of animals," the girl said when that story was finished. "Do you want to have a look?"

"Yes, I do," Hanne said.

"Here, here it is!" a boy said.

"I want to show her!"

"Here, look at the big fat cow!"

"I want to show her!" The little voice broke.

"You show to me, Muffin." Muffin? Was that really her name? "I close my eyes and you take me."

Close your eyes, Hanne used to say to her, I need to show you something special. How many times had she led a blind Oda or a blind Fritz by the hand into another room or across a playground? Like we were horses, Oda thought now.

"Okay, this way, this way," the little girl cooed. "Okay, turn in here." Their voices dwindled in the far room and Oda went back downstairs.

Hanne would have children someday. She would have her own family and these future people were the ones she would give her heart and her affection to. Oda would be the old lady they were forced to see on holidays then laugh about in the car on the way home. This right now was probably the closest they would ever be.

Oda tried to sit in her chair, but it wasn't like when Hanne went riding. She could hear footsteps, chatter, laughter. She could distinguish Hanne's deeper, slower voice from the children's, though she could not understand what they were saying. At the little girl's age, Hanne had loved cinnamon toast.

She went downstairs. Breakfast was over, the kitchen cleaned up. The innkeeper was gone, perhaps off on his bike. She cut four slices of her own bread, toasted and buttered them. In a cupboard over the stove she found cinnamon and mixed it with a few packets of sugar from a table in the dining room and shook the mixture onto the toast. She brought the slices on a plate up to the third floor.

"These smell good," Hanne said.

It was an apartment up here, with a living room and two bedrooms and light coming through many large windows. Hanne led her into a little galley kitchen. If she and Hanne ever came back here, this was the place to rent. But of course they would never come back.

"Yummy!" the older boy said. "Thank you for such a splendid treat." It was hard to believe this was the miscreant at the breakfast table each morning.

"Is it going all right, Hanne?" she asked in German.

Hanne nodded. Oda could tell she didn't want her to break the spell of English. But Oda didn't want to reveal to her or these children her rusty recall or her poor accent— she didn't have Hanne's musical ear—so she left.

She tidied their room a bit and sat back down in the chair with her book. She felt something warm on her feet. It was the sun, two squares of it lying across the floor. Out on the water it began to dance.

The Australians didn't come back at eleven thirty. Or twelve. At twelve fifteen she heard the phone ring up there, but she couldn't hear any conversation. Perhaps Hanne would need help making their lunch. Perhaps they would need some of her bread. Halfway up the stairs she heard the banging of the first morning. She guessed it was the big fat cow.

"Now it's twelve nineteen!" It was the older boy.

"Stop. My mother is below."

He didn't stop. "I don't have to do anything you say. You haven't even babysitted before."

"I did."

"No, you haven't. I heard your mum say."

"She doesn't know. I did before."

"Where. Are. My. Parents?" He gave a whack of the cow with each word.

The two other children were fighting over something.

"Stop it you both. Stop. Muffin has first, then you."

"She's had it all morning!"

"Where. Are. My. Parents?"

"You just like her because she's a girl. All girls everywhere are like that. They hate boys."

"I don't know where they are."

The banging grew louder. The children were screaming to be heard above it. Hanne tried to placate them one at a time with no success. Oda knocked but no one heard.

"Stop it! You must stop!" Hanne was yelling, too, now. "I will tell if you stop."

They stopped.

"Come sit," she said. "I have to tell you something I do not want to tell you."

Oda's insides went cold.

The children fought about who would sit where on the sofa. Above the arguing Hanne said, "Your mami and papi, they have died."

"No, they have not."

"Yes, they have."

"Like animals die?" the little girl said in a squeak.

"You're lying," the older boy said.

"The phone call," Hanne said.

"You said it was the innkeeper calling about our grocery order."

"I didn't know how you to tell." Her English was breaking down.

"They went to the caves. Just for a little while." His voice grew higher and higher.

"They have a bad guide who tooks them wrong. Too much water."

"They drowned in a cave?"

"Yes."

Once the older boy started to cry the others did, too.

"Come here," Hanne said. "Come up here to my arm. All of you. Come. Let me hold you."

Oda had gotten the call about the accident in the morning while Hanne was at school. She went to identify the body and sign the first batch of so many papers, as if death were just another business deal to push through. When Hanne came home she led her to the sofa and wrapped her arms around her and told her she had to tell her something she didn't want to tell her. Hanne had leapt up and run to her room. Don't tell me, she'd screamed. But Oda did. She sat on Hanne's bed. Don't touch me, Hanne said when Oda tried to stroke her hair. So Oda had sat in a chair beside the bed like a visitor in a hospital room. She'd ached to hold her. To be held. Let me hold you, she'd asked again and again.

She went up the rest of the steps. She knew she had to stop Hanne, but she was lulled into place outside the door by her tender voice, her soft cooing. "It's going to be all right. We will be all right. I will take care of you."

It was almost like hypnosis, like Hanne was playing Oda's part in a trance.

"Where will we live?" the older boy wailed.

"You'll come live with us."

"Here? In this house?"

"No," Hanne said. "But we can move here. Would you like? I could teach you to ride horse."

"I don't know."

"I'd like that," the girl said.

"I can teach you German. We will be fine."

From the foyer, Oda heard the Australians' voices. The wife said something and the husband laughed. Oda's limbs went cold, as if she were alone with ghosts.

They came up the steps quickly.

"Oda," the wife said. "I'm sorry we're so late. How did it go?"

Oda could find no words for them. But she didn't need to. The three children sprang out of the apartment, shrieking at their parents. Oda slipped around them into the apartment. Hanne was still on the sofa in the new bright light. Her skin had a feverish sheen.

Oda sat beside her.

"Mutti," Hanne said, and fell sideways and heavy into her mother's arms.

TIMELINE

My brother was helping me carry my stuff up to his apartment. "Just don't talk about *Ethan Frome*, okay?"

"What?"

"It's a thing of hers," he said. "She gets drunk and we fight and she says, 'Just because I haven't read *Ethan Frome*.'"

"Wait, seriously?"

We'd stopped on the landing. He could see how delicious I found this detail.

"C'mon. Just don't," he said.

If the situation were reversed, he'd be memorizing passages from that book already. "'Okay,' she said, quite reluctantly."

He made a noise that wasn't quite a laugh. "This may be a complete disaster."

We headed up the next flight. They were outdoor stairs, like at a motel. We dragged my garbage bags of clothes and books in. My room was straight through at the back. His and Mandy's was off the kitchen. I never went in there the whole time I lived there, so I can't tell you what it was like. From the kitchen, when they left the door ajar, it looked like a black hole. My room was bright with two windows looking out onto North Street, not the parking lot, and plenty of room for my desk. He thought it was funny I'd brought a desk. It was a table really, no drawers, with legs I had to screw back on.

I'd moved a lot but this time it was more like self-banishment. I didn't have the same feeling I normally did, setting up my room that night, twisting the legs back into the underbelly of the plank of wood and pushing it against the wall between the windows. That fresh start, clean slate, anything's possible feeling. I didn't have that. I knew I was going to write a lot of stupid things that made me cry before I wrote anything good on that table.

My brother came in and laughed at my only poster. It was a timeline of human history. It was narrow and wrapped around three walls and went from the Middle Paleolithic age to the Chernobyl nuclear disaster a few years earlier. It comforted me.

He put his thumbnail on a spot close to the end. "There I am. Born between the first manned spaceflight and the construction of the Berlin Wall."

We hadn't lived together since I was seven and he was thirteen. Now I was twenty-five and he was ancient. He sat down on my bed. "Does that guy know where you are?" he said.

"No."

"Will he find out?"

"Probably."

"Am I going to have to fight him?"

"More likely you'll have to listen to him sing 'Norwegian Wood' on the sitar under my window."

"Then I'll really have to beat him up."

"Your neighbors will probably beat you to it."

He laughed, hard. "They really fucking will." He looked around. "Mandy is not going to like all these books."

I didn't have bookshelves so I'd stacked them in columns in various parts of the room. They looked like a grove of stunted trees. "No *Ethan Frome* as far as the eye can see."

"Shut up. Now."

"Just tell her that," I said, louder. She wasn't even home yet. "Tell her I've never read it."

"No. We cannot mention it. Don't you get that?"

"I've never *ever* wanted to talk about *Ethan Frome* more than I do right now."

"She is going to fucking hate you." But he was leaning back against the timeline on the wall and laughing again.

I got a job at another restaurant, the most expensive one I could find. It was out on the way to Lake Champlain and farm country and didn't look like much from the outside but inside it was still a house, divided up into small rooms. Some rooms only had one table, some had a few. The restaurant was intimate. People came there for its *intimacy*. During the interview I was asked if I would be available to work graduation weekend, May 12 through 14, doubles if necessary.

"I can't give you this job unless you can promise me that," Kevin, the baby-faced manager, told me.

I promised. I was supposed to be the maid of honor at my friend Saskia's wedding in Massachusetts that weekend. In one of my unpacked garbage bags was the lilac dress she'd sent me to wear.

"Your brother is the kindest, most generous man," Mandy said. "I know because I'm an empath. My mother always told me, find the man with the biggest heart. Do you know, he scrapes the ice off my windshield every morning?" It was April in Vermont and still snowing some mornings, so we were not talking a few months of scraping. More like six or seven. That *was* kind of him. But her Wes and my Wes were entirely different people. My Wes was guarded, razor sharp, all edge. Her Wes was a "cuddle bear," so open, so *sweet*. Sweet was not a word we used in our family. Sweet was for suckers. Honesty, generosity, tenderness were not valued either. We had been raised to sharpen our tongues and defend ourselves to the death with them. We loved each other, we amused each other, but we were never unguarded, and we were never surprised by a sudden plunge of the knife.

Mandy was tall and sexy and worked as an assistant in a physical therapist's office because, she said, it was the place she'd been treated after "an accident in the home" when she was seventeen. Wes told me later her father had kneecapped her with her brother's baseball bat.

Wes and Mandy had no books. I couldn't even find a pen. That whole side of him—the awards at boarding school, the plays he wrote and directed in college until he dropped out—he'd buried to be with her.

I didn't see him much. He worked days putting electricity into ugly new houses on beautiful parcels of land, and I worked nights running up and down stairs, serving families in their best clothes and couples getting engaged in the small rooms. Kevin didn't fire me when I told him about the wedding in Massachusetts. But he was angry and put me on probation and made Tiffany give me the worst tables, the ones on the third floor. But we all drank together after the restaurant was closed, after we'd set the tables for the next night and tipped out the kitchen and bar. One night we all ended up on the floor of the Azul Room, the fanciest of all the rooms, the one where we put the governor and the provost of the university when they came in. We got into a big argument about something, the assassination of JFK, I think. We were all pretty drunk and shouting at the same time and Reenie, who'd studied child psychology but couldn't find a job, took one of the long, narrow porcelain vases off the mantelpiece—the Azul Room had a working fireplace and the waiter in that room always had to be stoking the fire on top of everything else—and said that only the person holding the vase could speak. She called it a talking stick, but I renamed it the Vessel of Power, and Kevin, who was trying hard to ignore me, laughed and I knew my probation wouldn't last much longer. I don't remember too many nights at that restaurant in Shelburne, Vermont, but I remember that one. I remember feeling happy among strangers, people I'd only known for a few weeks, which made me feel like things would be okay in my life after all.

At the last restaurant I'd worked at, in Cambridge, Massachusetts, I'd fallen for the bartender. Hard. I hadn't expected it. William was as quiet as his name and easy to work with. He wore vintage women's clothing to work, mostly Asian pieces—kimonos, sabais, qipaos—but on occasion a Chanel suit or a fluttering flamenco dress. He swept through the dining room in silks of sunflower yellow or scarlet red, delivering a bottle of wine or the gimlet you forgot about. He didn't seem to want attention for his clothing, and the one time I complimented an outfit—an embroidered turquoise sari—he thanked me curtly and said my six-top was waiting to order.

I ran into him at Au Bon Pain on a Sunday morning. He let two people go ahead of him so we could stand in the long line together. He was wearing men's corduroys and a wool sweater. Everything in my body shifted, as if it had known, as if it had been waiting. The way he put his hand in his pocket for his cash, the way he handed over the money and slid his coffee off the counter, the way he stood at the condiment stand and poured in some cream. The dresses had hidden the span of his scapulae, the narrowing of his waist, the hard muscles of his ass. Fuck. I'd heard he had a girlfriend. I left without milk for my tea.

He caught up with me, though, and we walked together with our hands on our hot drinks on the cold day. He asked if I'd seen the new sculpture outside Widener and veered into the yard to show me. We sat on the steps of the library and pretended we went to Harvard. "What's your major?" I asked him and he said "art history" and I said "me too" and he said "no way" and we tried to figure out if we had any classes together. We made up our courses: Hangnails in Modern Sculpture, Western European Scowls Versus Smiley Faces. Not surprisingly, he was good at getting into a role. I felt like I was in college again, that he was a cute boy I'd just met and he was about to kiss me. And he did. At 11:00 a.m. on a Sunday morning in November. It was the first time a first kiss made me want sex. Immediately. He looked at me like he felt the same and like it was nothing new. He relaxed against me, like my father sinking into the couch with his first drink. In the distance there was the sound of a little kid squealing, and William pulled away. It was a little boy, just entering the gates, running toward us. William took my hand. "C'mon." He tugged me down the steps toward the boy and the woman who trailed him. They were both dressed up, the boy in a silk bow tie and a tiny camel hair coat and the woman in heels and a black mackintosh and a flash of turquoise between.

"How is God?" William called.

"Good," the boy said, still running. It took a long time for him to reach us on his very short legs. "He's very good," he said crumpling his face into William's thigh.

He was still holding my hand when he introduced me to them, his son, he said, and his wife, Petra.

He insisted she didn't care, that their relationship had absolutely no restrictions, that they let each other be exactly who they were at any given minute. He always said that, *any given minute*, as if after sixty seconds you became someone else, wanted something different. I wished that were true. I only kept wanting him.

He liked to quote Ralph Ellison: "When I discover who I am, I'll be free."

He wore nothing under his dresses, it turned out. Up they came, so easily, in the handicap bathroom stall, the coatroom, the walk-in. Petra and I got pregnant the same month.

A robust month for my spermatozoa, he said. He loved it. He saw nothing wrong. My abortion made him sad, but he didn't argue and paid half.

In early April she came into the restaurant before we opened for lunch. She was only there a minute, handing him a set of car keys, but it was a warm day and I saw the curve of her belly below the belt of her wrap dress. I put down the tray of salt and pepper shakers and walked out. I called my brother, stuffed my crap into Hefty bags, and drove up to Burlington.

A week before Saskia's wedding, Wes and I made plans to go to the movies. I had a night off and Mandy was visiting her sister in Rutland. I met him at the bar he went to after work. He was in the corner, playing pitch with Stu, his work buddy, and Ron, the one who was always going into the hospital for his heart, and Lyle, who'd just gotten out of jail for a drug transport gone wrong at the Canadian border. I sat and waited for him to play out his hand. There was another guy at the table I didn't recognize. He was young, probably still in college. He and Wes were both chewing on toothpicks.

Wes won the trick with the jack of clubs.

"That's bull crap, Wesley Piehole," Ron said.

They all called him Wesley. He never told them his first name was Westminster. He got up to pay the tab.

"So how do you know Wesley?" the kid with the toothpick asked me.

"He's my brother."

The kid laughed.

Across the room Wes nodded toward the door and I followed him out.

A few days later he asked if I remembered the young guy from the bar. I pretended I didn't.

"College kid," he said, as if he'd never been one. "Lots of hair. He said he didn't believe you were my sister."

"I told him I was."

Wes smiled. "So you do remember him. He thought you were joking. About being my sister. I had to bet him a hundred bucks."

"Wes."

"All you have to do is come by the bar and show him your driver's license. When's your next night off?"

I gave him a look.

"C'mon. Easiest cash I'll ever make."

I went by. His name was Jeb. I brought my passport because the photo was better. He seemed bizarrely impressed by the passport, more impressed than a guy with a good haircut and a prefaded T-shirt should have been. For no good reason he showed me his license.

His full name was Jebediah. The photo must have been taken when he was sixteen. He looked like hope itself. He counted out five twenties for Wes.

"I don't know why you're smiling when I'm getting all the cheddar," Wes said.

"I thought you grew up under a rock, man. I thought you grew up out of the earth like a mushroom."

After I left, Jeb asked my brother if he could ask me out.

We went to a candy factory out of town on a hill— everything was on a hill or nestled in a valley there—on a Thursday afternoon. Three old ladies in plastic caps gave us a tour and we ate warm dark chocolate nonpareils and soft peanut butter cups from a brown bag on some playground swings. All the facts of my childhood enthralled him not because they had happened to me but because they had happened to Wes. Wes had put a bit of a spell on him. To him, Wes had crawled out from under his rock and appeared at the bar with tarred teeth and BO and riffing on everything from Hume to Hendricks, gathering the young and the old, the honest and the corrupt, the dead broke and the slumming elite. Jeb had grown up wealthy in Connecticut. He said his nickname prevented people from seeing the Jew in him. His brother Ezra had had a different and more difficult childhood. Jeb had had plenty of exposure to Wasps, but he'd never met one like Wes who'd repented, recanted, who said when pressed that he grew up in Lynn, not Marblehead, who would never admit to tennis trophies or snorkeling in Barbados.

In the apartment below us were Stacy and her three kids. They were wild and yelled a lot and sometimes you'd see Stacy in a big woodsman's coat, probably her ex-husband's, across the street smoking a cigarette with all three kids wailing inside. But I could tell she was a good mother. From my desk I watched her take the kids to school, and she'd walk like a duck or croon out a cheesy love song. Her kids were too young to be embarrassed, and I could hear them all giggling even after they'd gone around the corner. I wrote a few vignettes about Stacy and her kids at that desk, but they never turned into anything. She'd been out of work for a while and when she finally found another job it was the graveyard shift, cleaning at the hospital. She had to take it, she told Wes. If her husband found out she didn't have a job he'd try to overturn their custody agreement. After three months, she said, she could put in a request for daytime hours. So she made an arrangement with Wes and Mandy that if they heard anything they'd go down, and if the kids needed something they could come up. She left after she put them to bed and came back before they woke up.

The night after my date at the candy factory with Jeb—he'd kissed me at a stoplight and shot me little grins the rest of the way back—Wes, Mandy, and I were woken up by a piercing scream—a howl, really—like someone had been bitten by something. It was the youngest, A. J., who'd dreamt he'd been attacked by a kitten.

"Kittens can be terrifying," Wes said after he'd brought all three kids up to our kitchen and was heating up some milk. "They have very pointy teeth and if they are mean then their cuteness is even creepier."

Little A. J. was looking down at his hands on the table and nodding. His face was red and sweaty. The oldest looked like he wasn't really awake yet, and the girl was walking around saying about nearly everything in the room: "Mumma has one of these." Wes told her he needed help getting the honey from the high shelf and set her up with a stepladder and held her hand as she climbed to the top. When they all had mugs of sweetened milk in front of them, he reached for the salt and pepper shakers on the table and turned them into two friends named Willy and Nilly who were lost in the woods. By the end we all believed those small ceramic shakers were actual children, the way he made them move and speak and duck down when the eagles came looking for them, and that the toothpick he pulled out of his pocket was their mother come to find them. Mandy had tried to enter in with a spoon meant to be the father, but her voice was all wrong and I was glad when A. J. told her there was no father in the story and took the spoon out of her hand. We brought the kids back down and tucked them into bed.

The little girl looked at the clock on her nightstand. "Only three more hours till Mumma is back."

I stroked her forehead.

Her eyes flashed open. "How many hours did I say?"

"Just three," I told her.

We locked them in and went upstairs.

Sitting on the girl's bed, stroking her hair had made me feel breathless and too light, like gravity had stopped working properly.

I stayed awake until Stacy came back. I heard her front door open and shut but she was quiet after that, needing those couple hours of rest before she had to get the kids up. I fell into a deep sleep and when I woke up she'd already taken them to school.

I drove down to Saskia's wedding. I couldn't afford a room at the resort hotel, so I'd gotten out of the rehearsal dinner the night before. That meant I had to get to the church an hour early for some last-minute instructions. Someone named Caledonia met me at the church door. She made it clear she'd taken over my maid-of-honor duties. She'd even bought all the other bridesmaids—there were eight of us—sterling silver bracelets engraved with the date. It would have taken me several shifts at the restaurant to pay for just one of those bracelets. She gave me mine. The box was wrapped in a tight blue ribbon with a double knot. She waited for me to undo it and lift the lid. It was too big.

Bracelets always are. I have abnormally narrow hands. I slid it up close to my elbow and followed her to the nave.

Saskia was unrecognizable as she walked down the aisle. When we were kids she'd had this crazy electrocuted hair and now it was all smoothed down and folded into petals that splayed out like a peony and made her face seem very small. I wasn't sure if she was nervous or angry at me, but she only glanced over once and her expression did not change. I hadn't seen her in thirteen years. I suspect she chose me as maid of honor so she didn't have to pick a favorite among her real friends.

When it was over and the best man and I had walked back down the aisle, I saw William, not in the back but close to the front, on the groom's side, as if he were family. He was whispering with two aunties on either side of him. He was wearing a vintage white tux, absurdly overdressed for this afternoon wedding, but the cut was perfect and he so beautiful in it with his sheepish glance at me. He must have seen the invitation at my apartment in Cambridge before I'd left.

"Fuck him," I said.

"Another lovely touch, No Show," the best man said and detached my arm from his as soon as we reached the church doors. Caledonia had turned the whole wedding party against me.

As much as I wanted elegant William on my arm at the reception where everyone hated me, I told him to leave.

He brushed the back of his hand slowly up the side of my neck to my earlobe. "Let me just have a few hours with you."

"Please go." It was really hard to say these words.

A few of the other maids were watching but turned away when I came back across the parking lot. We got into limos that took us to a country club where we posed for photos on the golf course as the sun dropped, the light flat and orange across our faces, the way photographers like it. The entire wedding party minus me had gone to the same small college in Upstate New York. Saskia and Bo had met at freshman orientation. All the toasts contained words like "foretold" and "fate" and "meant to be." The women at least varied in height, weight, and hair color, but the men were enormous and indistinguishable, varsity oarsmen. Every time one stood up in the same suit to say the same thing the last one had said, I put him in a bloodred kimono or a lemon yellow wrap.

When I couldn't avoid it any longer I stood up and told a story about when Saskia was six and her dog got sick. When I sat back down everyone at my table was crying. Caledonia reached across and grabbed my hand. We had matching bracelets. After that people spoke to me and the elongated men asked me to dance. Saskia hugged me and said she loved me and we all threw birdseed at them when they left. They'd changed out of their wedding clothes and looked like they were going off to work in an insurance office. Someone told me they were catching a flight to Athens. I got a ride back to the church from a guy I'd had a crush on in high school. He pulled up next to my car and I could see him deciding if he had the energy to try something, but I slid out before he came to a conclusion.

On the way back to Vermont I thought about words and how, if you put a few of them in the right order, a three-minute story about a girl and her dog can get people to forget all the ways you've disappointed them.

It was close to two in the morning when I got home and all the lights were still on in our apartment. Mandy was having one of her episodes. I hadn't seen one yet. Wes had told me that every so often she drank herself into a sort of trance. I had laughed and said I couldn't wait, but he'd said it wasn't funny. She was pacing in the kitchen. Wes was at the table, which was covered with all sorts of bottles and glasses and mugs.

"Go straight back to your room," he told me. "Let me deal with her."

Mandy's head snapped toward me. She stopped moving. Her face was all rearranged, like this toy Wes and I once had with the outline of a man's face and a bunch of metals filings you moved around with a magnetic pencil underneath to alter his features and make him happy or sad or mad. Mandy was mad.

"There she is, Little Miss Scribbler. Little Miss History of the Fucking World."

"Here I am." I was sober and very tired.

"Dressed like a fairy princess."

I tried to curtsy but the bridesmaid's dress was too narrow. I looked like a misshapen purple mermaid.

Wes made a slight flourish with his finger for me to keep moving to my back room.

She saw him. She was too close to the drawer with the knives for my liking. But she said, "Baby, I love you so much." Her voice was empty of any emotion, like the identical oarsmen giving their toasts at the country club. "So much." She moved to where he was, stiffly now, as if her knees had never healed.

I hummed, very low, barely a sound, a few notes of "Psycho Killer."

He was looking at her as she came down heavily on his lap, but he heard me—or at least he understood without hearing me—and a tiny corner of his mouth flinched up though he was fighting it hard.

Mandy leapt up. "What's this?" She grabbed at the air over the table between Wes and me. "What is all this? I hate it. I hate it." She was fighting it now, some invisible swarm over the table. Her hand swiped at a glass and it went flying behind her, then more of the glasses and the bottles flew in different directions, and Wes just sat there waiting it out. When she stopped, she looked like she had so much she wanted to be hollering but it got stuck somewhere. The metal shavings of her expression rearranged again to a defiant brokenness.

There was tapping at the door.

Her head swiveled again. "I wonder who that could be," she said mechanically.

"Maybe it's Ethan," I said.

"Ethan who?"

"Ethan Frome." I moved to get the door before I could see her reaction.

It was William. In that fucking turquoise sari. He ducked. A Jim Beam bottle sailed over his head, skittered along the porch boards, slipped under the railing and smashed on the pavement below. He must have followed me three hours on the highway from the church parking lot.

Mandy came after me in her stiff-kneed way, but I quickly got around the table. She chased me, but the imaginary knee thing really slowed her down and I had to be careful not to go so fast that I caught up with her from behind.

"Are we playing Duck, Duck, Goose?" William said, coming into the kitchen.

"Oh fuck, is that your asshole?" Wes said.

"It is I," William said. "Her asshole."

"Definitely not what I expected."

"It's all very sexy under there, unfortunately," I said, still speed walking around the table.

Mandy stopped in front of William. "This is so intricate," she said, fingering the gold embroidery of his neckline.

Another knock on the door. William was closest.

"Hey man." It was Jeb. "Cool dress." He took in the room, saw me against the far wall. "Lucy," he said, his voice rising. He came over to me. "You're back." He kissed me. His lips were cold and tasted of smoke and pine. "I had this fear you wouldn't come back from Massachusetts. It was weird."

"You've been in the woods."

"Mhmm." He kissed me again. "Party." And again. "Bonfire." He was young. He didn't care who saw all the desire and energy he had.

"Petra had the baby," William said. "A little girl named Oriole."

It was the first time I'd felt alone in my body, like somebody was missing. I hadn't felt it before.

I don't know how Mandy knew—I hadn't told Wes about either of the pregnancies—but she came around so fast and held me tight.

The sirens came then. Two cop cars into our lot. Of course we thought they were coming for us, but they banged on the door below. They banged and they banged and Stacy's kids did not answer. We all stayed quiet. Wes shut off the light. Anything we said would get Stacy in trouble, he said.

Another car pulled into the lot. Stacy's ex. I'd seen him once leaving her place. But he never came when he was supposed to—on Sundays, his day with the kids.

We heard him outside with the police, talking at the door.

"It's okay, guys. Open up. It's me. It's your dad. It's okay. Michael, Allie, A. J." He said their names slowly and separately, like a new teacher would, like he was worried about mispronouncing them. "Open the door now." Nothing. Then: "Your mom knows I'm here. She's on her way. C'mon guys. Open up."

Wes called over to the hospital and told them to tell Stacy to come home immediately. Then he called downstairs. We could hear the phone ringing below and their father saying from outside: "Don't answer that phone!" And Wes breathed out, "C'mon." And Mandy said, "Everyone is so serious now," and we shushed her and she started to cry but softly, mewling.

The phone stopped ringing.

"A. J." Wes gripped the receiver with two hands. "A. J., listen to me. Your mom is on her way home. Don't open the door, all right? No, I know it's your dad but listen. Tell him not to, A. J. Tell him—"

But they opened up.

Wes yanked open our door and his feet went down those stairs fast as a drumroll. "You guys know there's a protective order prohibiting this man from removing those kids from the premises without their mother's consent. You know that, right?"

"I'm not taking them," the ex said. "They are." He pointed to people we couldn't see. We leaned over the railing. A man and a woman in street clothes were squatting down next to the kids, all three crying now, A. J. the loudest. He was trying to say Mumma but his lips wouldn't come together for the *m*'s.

"Who are they?" Jeb whispered.

"DSS," William said.

"No disrespect," Wes said, "but you are making a terrible mistake here. Stacy is coming right back. If anyone's at fault, it's me. She asked me to watch them and I had to run up to my place for another pack of cigarettes. There has never been a better mom. She loves those kids to pieces. She nurtures them and listens to them and— Look, here she is." He ran toward Stacy's car, just pulling in, and said loudly, "Stace, I was just telling them how I had to run up for another pack—"

It all got terribly tangled after that with Stacy sprinting toward her kids and the cops restraining her and the kids howling and hitting the DSS people to get to their mother and her ex suddenly losing it, calling her a fuck-hole and spitting in her face except that it hit the neck of the smaller cop, which he really didn't like and he let go of Stacy and shoved her ex up against one of the poles that held up the porch we were standing on and we felt the whole flimsy structure shake as he knocked him around. The cop knew he'd gotten on the wrong side of things and needed to make himself feel better.

Through it all Wes kept talking, as if a certain combination of words spoken in the right tone could make it all better for everyone. But the cops took the ex away and the children were buckled into the back of the DSS car. Stacy tried to run after it but Wes held her back. He yelled up for me to throw him his keys and got her in his truck, and they raced out of the lot to catch up with her kids.

William was still looking in the direction of the car with the kids in it, even though the building next door blocked the view of the street.

"Go home to your family, William," I said.

"I will," he said in a voice I hadn't heard before, solemn as a priest.

He went down the stairs and across the lot. He didn't have on the heels he normally wore with that outfit so the hem dragged a bit through the mud puddles.

Jeb ran the tips of his fingers along my temple and into my hair. He smelled like Vermont and everything I would miss about it later.

Mandy was still watching Wes through the little window next to the sink. "I found him, Mumma," she was chanting to the glass. "The biggest heart on earth."

Jeb followed me back to my room. He laughed at the grove of books and stepped up onto my bed in his boots.

I sat on my desk and watched him.

"Let's start at the very beginning." He put his finger on the first mark of the timeline: 200,000 BC, the appearance of Y-chromosomal Adam and Mitochondrial Eve.

My room smelled of woodsmoke. Wes and Stacy were chasing a car with her kids in it through the city. Mandy and I would wait up for him all night. And someday soon I'd sit at this desk and try to freeze it all in place with words.

Jeb held out his hand to me. "C'mere."

HOTEL SEATTLE

In college, Paul would buy a fiesta-sized bag of Doritos on Sunday after Mass and lie stomach down on his bed with his textbooks and notebooks propped up against his pillow and do all his work for the week ahead. He didn't stand up for hours at a time. A cup of coffee and a bag of Doritos was all he needed. Our dorm beds made an L in the room. Every Sunday I could look at his body for as long as I wanted.

We were best friends because we were roommates. I never deluded myself that he would have chosen me otherwise. Socially we balanced each other out. He was the guy who came into the room and everyone was relieved. I made people deeply uneasy, myself most of all. If we hadn't shared a room I would have been one of those guys on our hall that got a nod from him in the stairwell, maybe a bit of banter at the sink shaving, but no 2 a.m. arguments about transubstantiation or Bret Easton Ellis.

You grow up Catholic (mass, CCD, youth camps) with six brothers, a megalomaniac father, and a mother who is on her knees in prayer whenever you try to find her, it's hard to scrape through all the voodoo layers to recognize you're gay. "Sexual urges," Father Corcoran used to say through the permanent crust of his lips, "are the maggots at the feast." We learned to zap our urges the minute we felt them. And homosexual urges got snuffed even quicker, before they made it to the brain. They left a mark, though. I knew I was off somehow. For a long time I thought it was just religion I needed to flush out. That the girl in my arms was just not the right girl. I tried another and another. So many willing girls. And none of them quite right.

But on Sundays in college, with hours to trail my eyes up and down the length of Paul, who was quite narrow, with small, compact muscles in his calves and little fins for shoulder blades, the unearthing began. Proust had his madeleines and I my Doritos. Even now I can stick my nose into a bag of them and travel swiftly back to our corner room, the New England gloom and what felt at the time like a great tangle of feeling but was merely a boyish lust.

Without question, Paul was straight. He dated Marion Kelley freshman year, Ellie Sullivan, Bridgett Pappas, and Cheryl Lynch sophomore year, Lori Duff sophomore summer and straight up until the winter formal of senior year, where he met Gail McNamara, the very worst of the whole hit parade, whom he married two springs after we graduated, in 1987.

"I'm sorry you're not my best man. My mother made me choose Joe." Joe was the meanest of his brothers. "Otherwise he wouldn't have come home." He was fastening a yellow rose to my lapel in the basement of the church.

"Always a bridesmaid, never a bride." I was drunk from lunch. I was nervous. I had had sex—real sex—with a man for the first time a few weeks earlier. I knew I was gay. Finally. I could say it to myself without feeling nauseated. I also knew Paul was marrying the wrong person, knew every complaint he'd ever had about Gail. She treated him like an employee; she didn't always smell good; she was moody, irrational, not always honest, and used sex as a bargaining chip. I waited for him to crack, to beg me to help him bolt. We still had fifteen minutes before the ceremony.

"Are you sure about this?" I said finally.

"Yes. I've pinned on six of these already."

"No."

"Am I sure I want to get married?"

"To Gail."

He laughed. "I'm extremely sure."

A car of bridesmaids had pulled up. Their ankles and hemlines were at eye level through the small windows.

He wasn't even twenty-four. I said, "It's like you've walked into an enormous shop and chosen the first little tchotchke on the table."

He laughed. He had an amazing patience with people, even drunk people trying to derail his life at the last minute. "Gail is not a tchotchke. And she's about to be my wife."

He was devastating in his gray suit. A black line went down the outside of the leg and I wanted to touch it, trace it. I wanted to lift the coattail and have one last glimpse of the bum I looked at so primly, so reluctantly, the longing strangled deep inside me, for four years of Sundays. But now was not the time to tell my best friend I was gay and I wanted him. Now was the time to climb the basement stairs, to stand in a dark hallway, give him a dry, maidenly hug, and wish him Godspeed.

I told Paul last. First I told my mother (she said she'd tell my father herself, but I don't think she ever did), and then I told my brothers, one by one, in an elaborate fashion involving a letter and a gift and a surreptitious meeting in the telephone closet beneath the stairs one Christmas that will be mocked forevermore. *Pssssst*, is all one brother has to say to another, pointing to an imaginary telephone closet (my parents are both dead now, the house sold), and everyone is practically peeing their pants. For Paul I had no letter or gift or telephone closet. We used to meet a few times a year when his work brought him to Boston or mine brought me to New York, but I couldn't do it in person. He called me up one night (he was usually the one to call, late at night, some awful music on in the background) and when he'd gone on too long about his kid's strep throat, I blurted it out. "By the way, I'm gay."

He surprised me. He took it badly. He was silent, then grunted out a few measly sentences about being glad to have been told and got off the phone. He never called back. I lost him, just like that.

I got out of New England. I went to Seattle with my boyfriend Steve. I had been about to break up with Steve, but then he told me about a possible transfer to the West Coast. He was my first real boyfriend, and he'd been so generous and tender, helping to peel back all my prickly layers of fear and self-loathing, but I felt like it was time to move on, see what else was on offer.

Moving, resettling, making new friends, reconfiguring routes to coffee shops, bookstores, restaurants, clubs— all that can delay the end of a relationship indefinitely. We were still in that stage, our third year in Seattle, when Paul called.

Steve answered. We didn't have caller ID then, so phone calls were still a mystery. Steve started flapping his arm immediately, waving me up off the couch with huge sweeps while carrying on in a flat, placid voice, saying,

"Yeah, I think he's here somewhere. Unless he fell off the balcony into the neighbors' weed." Steve loved that we overlooked an illegal garden. He told it to everyone we met. "I hope you're not a cop," he added before covering the receiver with his palm and mouthing the words *Paul Donovan* over and over. Steve and I had been together eight years by then and though I'd tried to downplay my attraction to my college roommate, it was clear to me now that I'd hidden nothing.

During that whole short conversation, Steve was leaping from sofa to sofa, a mockery, a parody of my slamming heart.

Paul was coming to Seattle on business. He'd run into my brother Sean at a Red Sox game and he'd mentioned I was living out there. Did I want to have a drink next Tuesday night?

I went through the motions of checking the calendar and coming back to tell him I could get free.

He suggested 7:30 at his hotel.

"Great. I'll put it right on the calendar," I said, not knowing what was coming out of my mouth and Steve still hopping around me.

"You and your calendar," Paul laughed, as if this were a thing he'd known about me for years. "You won't remember?"

* * *

On Tuesday night I left Steve pouting in the apartment. He couldn't understand why he couldn't come along or at least meet us for dessert.

"We're having a drink, not dinner."

"Then let me meet you for the last drink."

"The last drink might be the first drink."

"Then let me just go to the bar, pretend to run into you. I don't have to be your boyfriend. I can be a coworker. I can be your masseuse."

"Like I want him to think I have a *masseuse*. It's bad enough I'm gay."

Steve shut his eyes and shook his head. "All the years your therapist and I have put into deprogramming you and it just doesn't make a dent, does it?"

"It's bad enough to *Paul* that I'm gay. It ruined our friendship."

"*He* ruined the friendship."

"Yes. Goodbye." I kissed him on the lips, which he liked. We weren't doing a whole lot of that lately. He held on to me and I let him, knowing that it increased the chances that he wouldn't follow me.

Paul was at the bar, elbows on the counter, looking over the bartender's head at a ballgame on the flat-screen.

"This place is like a morgue."

He turned to look at me. "Welcome to my world. Hotel bars and conference rooms."

He was middle-aged. His hair had retreated toward his crown, his shoulders had fattened and curled in. We didn't shake hands. I didn't want to. I busied myself with my jacket, made an unnecessary fuss about where to put it, and came slowly back to the chair beside him. It was anger that was making my heart thrash. I was still angry at him. Whether it was because he had dropped me or because he was no longer a god on earth but a middle-aged salesman, I did not know.

"But I like places like this," he said, shaking the ice in his glass. "Everyone drifting in from everywhere, from nowhere. Look at the woman in the corner. God, what is going to happen to her tonight?"

"A man in white polyester pants is going to walk in and spot her."

"The entertainment." He nodded to the corner, where there was a small stage with just a microphone on a stand.

"And he can just tell how good she'd be in duet."

"'I remember when,'" he began, falsetto. "'You couldn't wait to love me.'"

"'Used to hate to leave me.'" I couldn't help it.

"'Now after lovin' me late at night.'" We laughed. He could still hit the high notes. All the nights we'd sat on our beds with a beer and let our minds wander together like this. It wasn't like talking. It was effortless. Desultorating, I used to call it. Could he just slip back into that without an apology? Would I let him?

"Or," I said, "you could just go over there and fuck her yourself."

His eyebrows twitched down and quickly up. He wasn't going to show me his surprise at my bitterness. "I could indeed." He drained his drink. I felt him trying to think of something witty to add. At that moment, I felt like he couldn't have a thought or an impulse I couldn't anticipate.

"Do you travel for work?" he asked.

"No. Never." He didn't know what I did. "Clearly you do."

"Not as much as they want me to. It's not worth the battles at home when I come back. Gail is such a bean counter. A trip like this and I lose any possibility of an hour to myself for the next three weekends."

I didn't want to hear about Gail. I had given him the chance to defect. "So what do you do with an hour to yourself?"

"I don't know. It's all hypothetical. There is no free time. We've got three kids and a fixer-upper we never fixed up so I'm just managing the chaos dawn to dusk. Hardware store, pharmacy, soccer game. Repeat."

The bartender finally noticed me and came over. We knew each other from a party but neither of us acknowledged it and it created a tension Paul picked up on.

"What was that about?"

"What?"

"That little"—he rubbed his fingers together—"frisson."

"There was no frisson."

"There was a frisson. I know a frisson when I feel one."

"You might have felt a frisson. I was just ordering a Campari."

"A Campari. Is that some sort of code?"

"Code for what?"

"You know, a way to tell the bartender you're gay."

I stood up.

"Sit down," he said in a bored stentorian voice he must use with his kids.

"You owe me an apology, not further insult."

I saw his face flinch into an imitation and then flatten back out. I wondered if he did that to his kids, mimic them, the way my father had mimicked me. It was the first time I'd recognized the similarity between Paul and my father.

I should have left then.

But he said, "I do owe you an apology." And I sat, to wait for it.

We moved to a booth for dinner. We didn't switch to wine. He stayed with his single malts on the rocks, and I moved to flavored martinis. Neither of us had been very committed drinkers in college so the steady rate of his drink orders surprised me, as did my own insistence on keeping up with him. I had the sense that we were hurrying somewhere, having to get in our last meal and our last drink before we went, though for the longest time, idiot that I was, I didn't know where we were going.

We desulterated through the appetizers, horrible crab clusters covered in some sort of bark and fried to black. They inspired thoughts on food in New England—he lived in Cincinnati now—and between the two of us we recalled nearly every dish at the Boston College dining hall: the Welsh rarebit, the American chop suey, the pink sponge cake.

The waiter brought the entrees: osso buco, grilled salmon. I was full, buzzed, tired. My initial nervousness had collapsed into a heavy fatigue, laced with fear. I couldn't understand the fear, though I knew it had to do with the change in him. But I was used to changes. One of my brothers had recently lost over two hundred pounds, two close friends had had sex changes, and my mother, after my father's death, returned to college and became a large animal veterinarian. On her website she was listed as a stud service specialist. All Paul had done was become beefier and disillusioned—who hadn't?

"After you called that time, and told me, you know, what you told me," he said, and I didn't correct him about who had called whom, which was hard for me because I like people to tell stories accurately, "I must have spent a year just sifting through every memory I had of us. Shit, we went *camping*. We shared that foldout couch at my mom's apartment, showers, bathrooms. You had girlfriends! That little Carla or Carlie who was so in love with you. And that other one, began with a *b*. And didn't you have something going with Anna at my wedding? God, when I told Gail she was like, 'No shit, Sherlock,' but I tell you, I never saw it. You are one good performance artist."

"I wasn't acting. It took me a long time to put the pieces together."

"Oh, come on. That's bullshit. Everyone knows. You know it when you're six years old. You know if you're thinking I want to fuck *her* or I want to fuck *him*."

"You thought about fucking when you were six years old?"

"Damn straight. Miss Carlyle. Tight brown skirt."

"You knew what fucking was when you were six years old?"

"I knew Miss Carlyle and my penis had something going on. I knew that."

"Well, my penis didn't have anything going on with anyone until I was twenty-three."

"That is just not true. You had *girlfriends*."

"They were friends I made out with."

"You never slept with any of them?"

"No. And I never pretended to."

"I just assumed."

"I wasn't like you."

And now I figure out why I'm scared. I'm scared he's going to ask me if I wanted to sleep with him back then.

And I know I won't lie. And I know that will truly be the end for us.

"And now you sleep only with men?"

"Yes. One man at a time."

"You never had a ménage?"

Why do straight men love to ask this? "Not really."

"Not really?"

"Well, Steve and I once invited this guy up. We really thought we were going to do it with him, but then he took off his pants and he had this really flabby bum. He was a pretty slender guy with this white jelly bum and Steve and I could not stop laughing and he got mad—understandably—and left." Steve called it the big flabby fanny fiasco. We still could get laughing until our stomachs ached about it.

If Steve were here he could tell the story of that night so well no one would be able to breathe. But Paul didn't think my version was funny. "Is it better, sex with men?"

I laughed. "It is for me."

"I mean, sex is kind of athletic. I'm just wondering. I've kind of been thinking about this for a while. I mean. Women are always complaining about getting hurt, you know?"

"You mean emotionally?"

"No, physically. I mean sex hurts them."

"Really?"

"I mean, just when you get really into it they tell you it hurts."

"Really?" I didn't think there was much about any kind of sex that I didn't know about by now, but this news surprised me.

"I don't think I've ever had sex with Gail without her saying ouch like fifty times. I just wonder if with men it's different."

"Maybe it is. Some people are rougher than others."

"Are you rough?"

I realized he was leaning halfway across the table; his knuckles were touching my plate and his eyes, his watery, drunk green eyes, were all over me.

"Yes, kind of." It was the martinis talking.

"I already know what your penis looks like."

"And I yours," I said, trying for lightness and missing. The penis he'd mentioned was suddenly rock hard.

"I want to."

"Paul," I said.

He stood up, signaled to the waiter to put it on his tab, and nearly pushed me to the elevator. When it came we got in alone, and as soon as the doors closed he was at me—mouth, stubble, osso buco breath. I am kissing Paul, I am kissing Paul. His name rang through me like a cathedral bell. He pressed me hard against the brass handrail, his hands reaching for my fly, and then the elevator dinged, and he was on the other side of the box and looking like he'd never seen me in his life. But no one was on the seventh floor when the doors opened. He put out his arm for me to step out first and then he shoved me against the elevator opening and when the doors tried to shut they bumped against my back over and over, pushing me into him. He was at me like an animal, biting my nipples through my shirt, shoving, thrusting, as if he'd gotten a hold of a piece of meat too enormous to know what to do with.

"Paul." I took his face in my hands and held it in front of mine. "Slow down, baby. Let's get to the room."

He seemed unable to make eye contact but fished in his pocket for the key and led me down the hallway.

I stood in the center of the navy blue room as he locked and bolted and chained the door. I could hear him breathing. "You know, I think we need to take a few steps back here."

He didn't seem to register that I had spoken. He took off his shirt with one paw reaching behind his back and yanking up while the other fumbled with belt and zipper. His penis shot straight out at me and he was still breathing noisily but smiling now, proud of his erection, looking at me for the first time since we'd left the restaurant, as if he expected praise for what it could do.

"Lie down," he growled.

I sat on the bed. "I'd really like—"

"On your stomach."

"Paul, I'm not doing this."

Again his face flinched. Then he walked over and leaned down and kissed me, long and slow and gorgeous, just the way I knew he could, just the way he'd kissed all those girls I was so jealous of. But even as he was doing it, even as my own erection returned and my insides spun around, I knew he was placating me, giving me what I wanted but what he really had no interest in giving or receiving. And when he had weakened me enough, he flipped me over and yanked down my pants (they were Steve's jeans and slightly too big for me) without undoing them.

How many times that night did I try to make contact, beg him to slow down, to stop? He would not stop. When it was over, my body rang in pain. Paul passed out instantly, and I lay there waiting for the strength to get up, to return like this to Steve. It never came.

I woke up to the sound of the shower. I was sore everywhere. My legs and stomach had dark red bruises. I found it hard to roll over. "You sound just like Gail," he'd grumbled at one point when I complained about the pain. Is this how Gail felt in the morning? Is this what he did to her, or was it what he thought men did to each other, or was it simply what he did to me, to punish me?

The shower stopped. The faucet ran. The tap of a razor against the sink.

When he opened the door, his face was drained of color.

"Morning," I said sweetly, mockingly, the contented lover beneath the sheets.

He seemed not to be able to come into the room. "Do you have AIDS?"

"What?"

"I need you to tell me the truth. Are you HIV positive?"

"No."

"How do you know?"

"I've been tested plenty of times."

"Like when? When was the last time?"

"I don't know. Three years ago." It'd been more like five.

"Three years ago. Jesus Christ. Three *years* ago. I have a wife and *kids*. Fuck! I cannot fucking believe this." He went to the closet, unzipped a garment bag, and pulled a black suit and a striped tie off the hanger.

"Steve and I are monogamous."

He snorted. "Oh yeah. I can see that. Is he as monogamous as you?"

"Paul— This was obviously. This was the first. I've never—"

"I heard Steve on the phone yesterday. He seemed up for a fuck. Face it, guys, straight, queer, they fuck when they get the chance. And gay guys get a *disease* for doing it. And you know who's going to pay for it? My wife and my *kids*. You better fucking get out of that bed and go get yourself tested and send me the fucking results. Here, I'll get you a card and you can send it to my office. You hear me?" He was rummaging around in his briefcase, which was on top of his suitcase. "What the *fuck!*" And he tipped the whole thing over, briefcase, suitcase, stand. They crashed against a little round table that held a small vase of tulips and when the table didn't quite fall he pushed that over, too. Slowly I moved toward my clothes.

"I thought you guys were supposed to wear condoms."

"I wouldn't say I had a whole lot of choice about that last night."

"What is that supposed to mean?"

"It means that your train was going into the station and there was nothing I could do to stop it."

Then his pale-blue face knotted to one side. I'd never seen him cry. It never occurred to me Paul could cry. He stood there with a white towel wrapped around his thick waist, his hairless fat chest heaving, and his face all crumpled like a dirty napkin.

I continued to dress. Every movement hurt in some way. He wanted me to comfort him, to acknowledge his strange premature straight man's middle-age crisis. Maybe he even wanted to have sex again.

I unchained and unbolted the door and left. The corridor was silent. The elevator ascended, opened, accepted my weight with only a slight sag. It dropped with a swift, gentle sigh to the lobby.

In a red leather chair by the revolving door, Steve was sleeping. I nudged his knee with my knee and his eyes opened and I watched them find the whole story in my face. He was older than me and wise as God. He walked beside me, very slowly, as slowly as you can imagine walking, out onto the street, over to Pike, and all the way back home.

WAITING FOR CHARLIE

Everyone had told him to speak to her like normal. But how could he, when her shaved head slumped toward the window away from him, when the hospital smock had loosened, revealing a chest freckled and flat as a washboard with her large breasts fallen to the sides, when she lay propped up beneath a sign that read: PT DOES NOT HAVE BONE ON RIGHT SIDE OF SKULL.

They had removed it because of inflammation after the accident. Otherwise, she would have died. Now, weeks later, the swelling was down and the side without the bone had caved in like a rotten melon. He'd grown used to his own deteriorations: his hip, his lungs, his skin that tore like wet tissue. He had to sleep with oxygen. He bled for no good reason through his clothes. But looking at this child, not even twenty-five, so badly damaged she had not yet surfaced to consciousness, was not something he was ever going to get used to. He would never come back here again. Never.

Like normal.

"Hello, Charlotte." He waited for her to turn and greet him. Of course he knew the circumstances, but when, in the past ninety-one years, had he spoken to someone in a quiet room and not had them respond?

He spoke louder. "I said, 'Hello, Charlotte.'" He was certain that within the hour he was allotted he would snap her out of it. He had accomplished far greater things than that in this lifetime.

He knew his grandchildren were scared of him. Or had been. He'd been big and loud. He hadn't liked their gum chewing or their back talk. He felt sorry now for all the times he'd told this one her hair was too short, that it was bad enough she called herself Charlie. But sometimes direction was what children needed.

There was a chair by the window. He pulled it closer and sat.

"This is your grandfather, Charlotte. I've come down by myself to see you. I want you to wake up now. You've gotten everybody too worried about you." He remembered his wife telling him not to say anything negative and added: "You're a very good actress but come on now."

There was a loud cracking noise, like something hard and brittle splitting in two. He saw the wide mouth of a tube resting on her collarbone. He recognized the contraption from his last operation. It pumped into the air fifteen percent more oxygen, and it had made him feel safe. It didn't seem to be rubbing against anything but the washcloth underneath. Her jaw shifted and there was another crack. It came from inside her mouth.

"Hey, don't do that." He put his hands on her cheeks. Her skin was slick with sweat. Beneath his fingers, her chin swayed once more from one side to the other, releasing the terrible sound. He was frightened he'd find every tooth in pieces, but when he pried open her mouth, they were all fine. They were even familiar. She'd spent a whole summer with him, the summer her older sisters went to camp and her parents divorced. She was eight and all her teeth seemed to be falling out or growing in. Nearly every night, she showed him the latest developments. She'd been a nervous child, but she'd grown into a bold, confident young woman. Overconfident, perhaps. All his grandchildren were overconfident. When he complained of this, of their aggression and recklessness, he was laughed at. *The pot calling the kettle*, they said.

He'd seen a picture of the trail she'd fallen on. "I wouldn't have gone down that slope. It was too steep and too icy and you could see the rocks were bare. It was a foolish thing." He didn't care. She needed scolding. She was probably sick of people coming in cooing and mooning and pitying her. She needed a firm hand. "A very foolish, stupid thing."

On a whiteboard facing her bed, facing the sign about her skull, her sisters had written in Magic Marker: "Good Morning, Charlie! It's Saturday Feb. 15. You've had a skiing accident. We're all at Dad's and will be back soon. Can't wait to see you!" All over that wall were photographs, posters, drawings, poems, and letters. There were red roses and a slew of valentines on the radiator.

In a basket on the windowsill beside him were several glass bottles. One was full of little red beads. He turned it around and the label said WHOLE RED PEPPERS. The others were liquid: SEAWATER, GRENADINE, VINEGAR.

"How are you all doing?"

A nurse was in the doorway. He tried to think if there was anything he needed, then remembered he wasn't the patient.

She glanced down at the basket in his lap. "Were you thinking of giving her a little aromatherapy?"

"No."

"Well," she said in the way nurses did, thoroughly inured to resistance. "Her therapist doesn't come on Sundays so it might be a good idea. All you do is remove the cap and let her take in a few whiffs. Smells are amazing. They trigger memory quicker and deeper than any other kind of stimulant to the senses."

He chose a bottle whose label had been peeled off. He unscrewed the cap and the smell of lemons flooded the room. He breathed it in eagerly. It was a beautiful smell. He thought of his three granddaughters in the summer, placing rusty lawn chairs in the yard and squeezing lemons into their brown hair. After the divorce, they often slept over, though his son's apartment was only a few blocks away. They said the beds were more comfy. He put the bottle beneath her nose. There was no reaction.

"Do you remember Dennis Wight, Charlotte? He was asking about you the other day."

Once he had found Dennis on one of the lawn chairs in the middle of the night, snoring loud enough to bring down the house a story. The boy had been waiting for a glimpse of Charlie through a crack in the guest bedroom's curtain.

"You girls used to get so tan. And your hair had streaks of gold." Without looking, he could feel the bleakness of February through the window, the half-frozen mud puddles in the parking lot below. "Summer is a beautiful season, Charlie."

"It sure is."

He had forgotten about the nurse. He wasn't sure what he'd said and what he'd just thought about. He put the cap back on the lemon and brought out the peppers. No smell was released. He brought them to his nose. Still nothing. He shook the bottle and smelled and his head exploded. He coughed and wheezed and wiped his eyes with a handkerchief. During all this the nurse laughed. He wished she would go to hell.

He held out the bottle for Charlie. Again, she breathed lightly without response. In the war he had seen plenty of death, but never in all his years had he seen something as terrifying as this face before him now. All of its muscles had gone flaccid. The flesh was like jelly. Her chin pooled onto her neck; her cheeks flopped back near her ears. Even her nostrils had flattened. Physically, she had lost everything that had once defined her. He looked away, down at his own legs. His old brown pants billowed out like a skirt; the cuffs dragged on the ground. His belt, the leather worn thin on the first notch, was now fastened at the last one. Soon he would have to puncture a new hole. They were both adrift from their bodies. And without the body, what are we? Had he ever truly believed in a soul?

He shook the bottle hard and kept shaking until he heard her take a breath. It made him sneeze four times, reminding him of sunlight and pollen and dusty books, but it had no effect on her at all.

The summer her parents divorced, she'd walked from room to room complaining of boredom.

"Aren't you bored in there, Charlie? Aren't you horribly bored by this coma?"

The nurse reached over the bed and put a hand on his arm. "Don't."

"Am I not allowed to say the word 'coma'? Is that a dirty word around here?"

"It could frighten her."

"Well, she's frightening me." He hadn't heard himself whine like that since he was a little boy.

"Maybe it's time to go now."

"No. Not for me. It's not time for me to go." He felt how fast his heart was beating and knew he had to calm down. He rummaged through the basket and found a bottle of blue liquid marked AFTERSHAVE. He opened it and breathed in dances when he was young: the bathroom of his parents' house, his brother, Tom, hogging the sink, and the smell of his own cologne in the hair of a girl at the end of the night. He had never been religious, but he knew that if anything happened to Charlie, Tom would be waiting for her. They would be about the same age now. Tom was only twenty-four when he died. It seemed impossible that he had lived sixty-seven years without him.

He feigned another coughing fit and wiped his eyes. It was too much. There was too much unnecessary loss. There always had been. He held the aftershave up to Charlie's flat nose. She took it in slowly, and opened one eye. The pupil rolled down and she looked straight at him. He was too dumbfounded to greet her. Here she was. He had done it.

"That happens," the nurse said. "Only that one eye. Around and around."

Obediently, the eye began to travel the length and breadth of the room. When it swung back around to him, he waved and smiled as if for a camera. No one knew, not even the specialists with their fancy jargon and machines, if Charlie was still in there.

He put the blue bottle back and idly fished through the basket again. He wasn't sure he had the stamina for another and was relieved when the nurse suggested that three was plenty for one session.

"Those were neat smells, weren't they, Charlie?" she said before she checked her vital signs and left.

Her presence had been an annoyance, but the room seemed drained and vacant after she left. He took his granddaughter's hand, a hand clenched tight on her chest, and tried to pray. He'd never learned to pray. All he knew how to do was beg. He begged for this child to be spared, but even in the small chamber of his own head, his voice was faint.

He sat back in the chair. He hadn't noticed the enormous clock opposite him. He still had forty more minutes.

Footfall was steady outside in the hallway. Occasionally a nurse or orderly would slow and glance in, having been informed about the very old man visiting in room 511.

"I am an arrogant man," he whispered. "I thought this would be easier."

It was a nice room, bigger than any he'd had here. There was something comforting about hospitals now. He liked the ambience, the voices on the intercom system, calling out names of strangers, the steam coming out of the oxygen tube, the bright light of the buzzer near the bed, the rolling of carts and chairs in the hallway, the clean sterile smells. He felt safer here than at home where accidents were waiting, where help was across town. Here, death felt far, far away.

The chair was comfortable. A light rain began to tap at the window. He could feel the extra oxygen in the room and took it in gratefully. Sleep came over him, thick and slow, and just before he surrendered to it, he felt the rhythm of his breathing falling into Charlie's, falling into an easier, simpler place where they might finally reach each another.

MANSARD

F rances flew out to greet her.

"Audrey!"

They all had names like that then, out of old storybooks.

"Why didn't you answer your phone?" Frances said.

"When did you call?"

"Five minutes ago."

"Well, I was driving here, wasn't I?" Audrey had never seen Frances so wild. Out in the gravel without shoes. The bottoms of her stockings torn, most likely. Hair in tufts in the back. "What is it?"

"I have to cancel. I'm sorry."

Audrey looked toward Frances's house. It was new, hideous. But inside there were framed articles about its architect hanging on the walls. Audrey's Larry said it looked as if someone had taken a sledgehammer to a perfectly good house and scattered the bits.

"Is someone sick?" Audrey said.

Frances had four children, each with their own separate "module" for a bedroom. Who knew what they would get up to when they were teenagers.

"No." Frances was holding one red shoe. "My father showed up."

"Your father?"

"I got a hold of Elinor but I couldn't reach— Oh."

It was Sue, checking her lipstick in the rearview as she pulled in, veering away just in time.

"You nearly killed us!" Audrey felt a sort of wildness herself now, a hysteria she would for once like to give in to.

Sue got out of the car in a new suit, baby blue plaid.

The suit calmed Audrey. She'd helped Sue on the phone last week decide about it. "It's darling," she said, plucking the sleeve before they kissed. "Bridge is off, I think, Suzie."

"What are you talking about?"

They never canceled Friday bridge. And it had only been cut short that once, two years ago at Audrey's house, when Larry had called home and told her the president had been shot in Dallas.

"Bridge is definitely off! Everything's off!" Frances said. She was tearing out the grimy insole of her red pump.

"Her *father's* here," Audrey said.

Sue looked around for an unfamiliar car. "How'd he get here?"

Of all the questions to ask.

"I don't know," Frances said.

"The train? A lift? Did he bring luggage?"

"Sue," Audrey said.

"No." Frances turned toward the house. "No luggage. I have to go in now. He'll be watching. You all should go."

"We're staying," Sue said. "Aren't we, Auds?"

Frances had spoken of him only once, three years ago at Sue's house when their afternoon tea had bled into cocktails and Sue's housekeeper had taken all the children up to the bath. They were talking about their parents' marriages, how they were trying to do things differently. Upstairs the children were shrieking. Audrey worried about them getting too wound up and hitting their heads on the edge of the tub. Frances said that her parents were divorced. Audrey had never known anyone with divorced parents. They split before the war, Frances said. In '39, when she was three. She had no memory of them together. *How awful,* Elinor said. And Frances said, *No, it was for the best.* Her father was dangerous. He had aliases. *A spy,* Frances said. A double agent. Maybe a triple agent. Audrey wondered if she was making that up. A triple agent? Frances had heard him one time on the phone when she was very young, she said, speaking a foreign language. She didn't know which one. Just that her father had turned into a different person. He had no idea I was in the room watching. His whole face changed when he spoke. My mother hadn't let my sister and me see him again till we turned thirteen. Then we were allowed once a year to have lunch with him in a park in Maryland, an hour from our house. My mother made the lunch. Always the same thing, tomatoes and cream cheese with chives. There was never a scene. He came down a path and left the same way. He came to my wedding reception, briefly. Stood in the back. Didn't make a toast or ask me to dance. I haven't seen him since, she said.

"Papa?" Frances said in the vestibule, if you could call it that. It was more like the lobby of a small museum. Her voice echoed from all directions, magnifying the panic.

"In here," came a voice, quiet, with a lilt of anticipation. Audrey followed it. The others—even Frances, who should have known the way sound traveled in her own house—were uncertain where it had come from. The lobby branched off in four directions, like four legs of a spider. Audrey moved down the back right leg into a den she'd never seen before.

Frances always entertained in bright rooms, the formal living room or the dining room or the sunroom beyond the kitchen, but he had set up the bridge table in here, in this small dark room. Audrey was aware of clutching her clutch, of the two beads of the clasp boring holes in her finger and thumb. He was counting the deck. He glanced up, down, immediately up again. The cards kept flowing fast through his hands. He smiled, eyes back down, shaking his head. "You made me lose count," he said, barely audible.

The others caught up behind her.

"What's all this?" Frances said, the way she would to one of her children if they'd made a mess.

"Do not ever let it be said that I broke up a bridge game."

"Oh, Papa, no."

Audrey couldn't get over the *Papa* bit. From another century, or country.

"We can take our coffee in the sunroom."

"I'd like to play. I haven't played bridge with you since you were—"

"We never played bridge, Papa. Not once." But she took the seat to his left.

Which meant that Sue had to sit down opposite her, because they were always partners. Which put Audrey facing Frances's father.

He gave her a slight somber bow, though he was seated.

"Papa." She couldn't stop saying it, as if she'd been denied a candy and was now cramming them into her mouth. "This is Audrey Pennet and Susan West."

"Ben Yardley," he said to Sue and put out his hand.

"Pleasure," Sue said coolly. She liked fighting other people's battles.

He turned to Audrey. "Partner," he said. His hand was small and warm. She watched it join the other to deal. Small quick hands.

She wasn't lucky in cards. She never fanned them open and saw anything spectacular. She wasn't that kind of person. Fortunately Elinor, her usual partner, was. So was Sue. And even Frances on occasion had a good streak. Audrey was the B actor of bridge. She had learned to play her mediocrity well.

He dealt her an extraordinary hand.

She hardly knew how to contain herself. She quickly added up the points. Three aces, two kings, a queen, a jack. A void in diamonds. Eight spades. Twenty-five points. She kept her eyes down. But oh how she wanted to look up and let him see it in her face.

He bid one heart. Perfect. The only suit she didn't have an ace in.

Sue bid one no trump. Audrey bid two spades. Frances passed, Ben passed, Sue bid two no trump.

"Five spades," Audrey said. She hoped not too loudly.

"You're insane," Frances said. "Double."

Ben was the dummy and she played the round easily, feeling his approval without having to search for it.

"That's my girl and a half," he said when she took the last trick. It was something her own father used to say. Girl and a half.

They played out the rubber. Each hand was like Christmas. The aces and face cards sparkling at her like jewels.

"Why don't we take a coffee break?" Sue said. "And maybe switch things around when we come back."

He lowered his eyebrows conspiratorially. "They're trying to break us up, Audrey."

The kitchen was filled with sun. They squinted at each other as Frances moved briskly about.

"I'll get the cups," Audrey said, opening the cupboard.

"No, I want to use the Spode."

"Where are they?"

"I'll get them, Audrey," Frances said, sharp, the way she spoke to the son she didn't like much.

Sue had gotten the sugar and was filling the little pitcher with cream. Ben had wandered down the hall past the sunroom. Audrey found him at the end of the spider leg, in Cassie's module. Cassie was the youngest and the farthest from her parents' bedroom, which was down past the den.

"You passed the sunroom," Audrey said from the doorway.

"It appears I have grandchildren," he said, touching a copy of *Madeline* on Cassie's unmade bed.

"Yes, you do." She felt a flare of anger at him. Her own father had died a month before her first child was born. He'd written a letter to that unknown grandchild in a cursive jagged with pain. It struck her as more poignant now, that letter, than it ever had before. She had been so consumed by her own loss that she'd barely considered his. *Though I will never cast an eye on you*, he'd written, *I will always love you, all your days.* He had anticipated the end of his own ability to love anyone. When you die, she thought now, you can no longer give love. You can't give love anymore. She wouldn't be able to love her children. It struck her suddenly as the very worst thing about death, worse than not being able to breathe or laugh or kiss. A kind of existential suffocation, to not be able to give her children her love anymore. She thought of Larry. There would come a day when one of them would not be able to give the other love, when one would be alive without the love of the other. But this didn't feel as dramatic.

Ben was still touching the book. But he was watching her.

"Papa!" The panic was back in Frances's voice. "There you are. Don't look at Cassie's room. It's a mess."

"It's a pristine and perfect room," he said, not even pretending to look away from Audrey.

In the sunroom they drank coffee in the white Spode cups. The sun shone through Ben's hair to his scalp. Sue led them into silly conversations. Beach club membership rules, Bonwit's new charge card.

They went back and played another rubber, Frances with her father. They didn't have the cards but Sue let them win, bidding low, passing unnecessarily, making mistakes. Sue wanted Frances to have Audrey's experience of a victory with him. But Frances was not his girl and a half. Audrey felt him beside her, felt the heat of his arm though it never touched hers, felt his eyes on her hand when she played a card, felt they were speaking the whole time, though later she would wonder what on earth she thought they were saying.

She hoped Frances would invite them to stay for lunch as always. It was past one by the time the second rubber was finished and she was starving. But she didn't. She was ushering them out. She had two hours alone with her father now before the kids came home. They left the den and moved toward the light. Audrey would be expected to say her goodbyes and drive away. It was like discovering a sun and being expected to move in the opposite direction. She wanted at least to have her own goodbye. She said at the very last moment, just as Sue went out the door, that she had to use the ladies' room. There was one just off the kitchen but she went to another one, the one near Molly's module. It smelled of middle school perfume, lemon and lilies. She took her time.

He was still in the lobby when she returned, looking at an article on the wall, "Modern Magnificence," about the house. She could hear Frances in the kitchen, washing the cups by hand.

"Goodbye," Audrey said, without conviction.

He took her arm and brought her to the glass windows that looked out at the pool, already covered for winter, where Frances could not see them from the kitchen. His lips were like his hands, plump and warm, wetter than she had imagined. He took her lower lip in his teeth and tugged gently. He moved to her cheek and let out a moan in her ear. She felt him grow hard against her.

"Papa?" Frances called from the kitchen.

They pulled away.

"Is it a secret, where you live?" she said quickly.

His grin blossomed. "Of course not. Graham Street. Portland, Maine."

Frances had taken off her shoes again and she came around the corner without sound. "What's in Portland, Maine?"

"Just a place I lived once. I was on the second floor, above a sort of grimy hair salon. It was an old sea captain's house that had been broken up into apartments. Not a very wealthy sea captain, I don't think, no view of the sea. But a pretty mansard roof." He'd stuck his hands in his front pockets, pulling out the fabric casually, reminding Audrey of boys in her youth after close dancing.

"I didn't know you'd lived in Maine," Frances said.

"No?"

"No."

"Thank you for today," Audrey said and kissed Frances on the cheek. She glanced briefly at him. "Nice to meet you." She tried to make it as flat and bland as she could, as if they were really saying goodbye.

*　*　*

It wasn't easy to drive two hours north and two hours home while her kids were at school without anyone noticing her absence. The first time she did it, Becky threw up at recess and had to go to Elinor's house because no one could reach Audrey. She said she'd been shopping and lost track of time. Another time, Russell hit his head against a desk and had to stay on the cot in the school office for hours. "Where were you?" he wailed all the way home. And then in December, Larry came in from the garage and asked how in the heck the new Mustang had gone nine thousand miles already. She felt the blood drain, but he laughed and said, You head down to Atlantic City every time you drop the kids off? And she saw he didn't expect an answer.

That first time, she didn't even know what she was looking for. She just drove up and down Graham Street, two and seven-tenths miles, believing she would just know it. Had he said a number when he'd said Graham Street and she'd forgotten it? Old sea captain's house, he'd said. Not wealthy. No view of the sea. Hairdresser on the bottom floor.

It was only driving home that she had remembered the roof. A kind of roof. It began with an *m*. She didn't know roofs. She casually asked Larry one night coming home from a dinner party about the kinds of roofs there were.

"Well, you can make a roof out of slate or asphalt shingles or tile . . . or even grass like in Sweden."

"No, *styles* of roofs." Her arms burned in impatience. "Use the technical term. Be technical."

"Do you need to take another tranquilizer, Auds?"

"A kind of roof that begins with an *m*." She was nearly crying.

But he didn't know.

She went to the library. It took all of five minutes.

Mansard.

Not one mansard roof on Graham Street in Portland, Maine. Mansard. It sounded French. It seemed French, like the houses in *Madeline*.

At a New Year's Eve party, Frances said her father had been with them for a few days over Christmas.

"What a riot that man is," Elinor said. "Why weren't you there that night? Were you out of town?"

"Yes, we were visiting my mother," Audrey said, low so Larry wouldn't hear.

"I gave him the new Greene novel," Frances said. "He loves Graham Greene."

Madeline. Mansard. Graham Greene. It was clearly a puzzle she was meant to solve. She tried. That winter she drove up and down Green Street, Greenleaf Street, Greenwood

Lane, Madeline Street, French Street, Queen's Court. She had a babysitter with a license who could pick up the kids at school now, so she didn't have to worry about time. She found a few mansard roofs, but they were mostly single-family houses. The two that weren't had women's names above the second-floor buzzers, no hairdressers on the bottom floor.

But she liked driving through the neighborhoods at dusk. She could see it so vividly at that hour, the tall house with the French roof, the hair salon closed for the evening, everything dark save the band of light around its middle, the second floor all lit up and glowing, waiting for her arrival.

SOUTH

They head south, and as they move out from under the dense Baltimore sky toward air and ocean and hot sun, Flo and Tristan beg their mother, Marie-Claude, to tell stories. Flo loves the ones about when Marie-Claude was as young as she is now, and Tristan wants to hear, over and over, how he was born.

Because Marie-Claude does not want her children to talk about their father, who left her at the end of last spring, nearly a year ago now, she gives them the stories they ask for. She tells Flo about Alain Delor, her first crush, and Tristan about the market in Paris where her sac broke as she stood buying peaches in the rain.

But when she begins the story about her first dance, Flo interrupts her. "What about the ghosts in Austria, Mom? Is there one about some ghosts at a fancy ball?"

Marie-Claude shakes her head, certain she has never told either child that story.

Using the headrest, Flo pulls herself up closer from the back seat. "Yeah, there is." Some of her mother's fine hair tangles around her fingers, sticky from candy.

"That hurts, Florence," she says. "Dammit," she adds in English.

"Maman!" Tristan says, truly shocked to hear an American swear word out of his mother's mouth.

Marie-Claude is surprised, too, and a bit alarmed by the sudden swell of anger. She had promised herself no harsh words to Flo today.

She looks at the enormous clock beside the speedometer: four more hours. She wonders if Flo or even both of them should have gone with their father to New York instead of coming with her to Hatteras. She cannot predict her moods or the size of Bill and Karen's house or whether Tristan and Flo will like her friends' children. She wishes she had enough money to fly them home to Lyon for Easter. She takes her eyes from the road to the fields beside them, a movement as welcome as straightening her legs might be. She wishes she could go on looking sideways.

Tristan says, "What story about ghosts in Austria? Watch the road, Maman. What story about ghosts?" She knows he will persist, never forget, not for one day of their vacation.

"It was in a castle," Flo says, "a really old spooky castle that used to be a big deal, like a king or a count used to live there or something. And Daddy was there. I think they were engaged then. Were you engaged to Daddy then? Please tell it, Mom."

This is new, Flo calling her Mom instead of Maman, and Marie-Claude hates it.

She wonders how Flo can know about Austria. Sometimes it feels there is nothing about her life her children cannot uncover, cannot redefine. Once she had thought there would be a certain amount of grace and mystery in being a parent and that what went unsaid about her experiences would be respected and what was revealed would be absorbed without contradiction, occasionally sanctified. Wasn't that how she had treated her own parents' pasts? Perhaps it is because they have become American, these children of hers.

"You two tell me stories. I'm tired of talking."

"No," says Flo. "Tell the ghost story. Please, Mom, please. Please!"

Tristan joins in, and Marie-Claude lets them continue far past the point at which she'd assumed they'd stop, until their chanting unsettles her more than the idea of telling another story. "Okay," she says. "Okay."

"Your father wasn't with me then," she begins. "I hadn't even met him." She tries but fails to conceal the pleasure she takes in this fact. "I went with my cousin

Giselle. She had been invited by her best friend at boarding school in Lausanne, Sigrid. The ball was just outside Linz at a palace that had once belonged to a Habsburg archduke, Franz or Friedle or someone, one of Francis the First's sixteen children. The palace was later confiscated when the imperial family was forced out of the country by the new government. Eventually, it was resold to this Sigrid's grandparents. I didn't know much of the history. I just knew that Giselle traveled with a pack of rich friends and that Sigrid wasn't the only one who could throw a party in her own castle. And I was a bit more like your father then. I loved big houses and beautiful clothes."

"He does not," Flo says, but even in her irritation at one of her mother's jabs, she can't muster up enough conviction to pursue an argument. She has already begun to notice how her father seems more pleased when she plays at Janine's house with the pool than at Bree's apartment.

Marie-Claude instantly regrets the comparison, regrets this mood on the first day of their trip, and rushes on. "My date was one of Sigrid's cousins, a sullen boy who seemed to want to talk about nothing else but the strategical blunders of the French army. His country gets occupied twice during one war, and he has the nerve to bring up the failure of the Maginot Line! But I didn't really care. I was at a ball in a fancy dress and could laugh at just about anything."

Flo marvels at the thought of her mother (whom friends call a slob, who always wears her hair yanked back with the brown rubber band off the newspaper) in a ball gown, patiently humoring her date. Flo is beginning to question these images her mother feeds them of her disposition before she married their father. She always makes herself out to have been giggly and lighthearted, the gravity of life never pulling on her until she found herself married with children to raise. But her mother's face is serious, has always been serious, her expression in even the most spontaneous childhood photographs resembling, as her father once said, the portrait of a disgruntled cabinet minister.

Slowly, the story begins to make Marie-Claude feel better as she describes the carriage they rode in, the view of the Danube, the black horses in the twilight. She senses her children's full attention, Flo's syrupy breath near her ear and Tristan's small body turned sideways toward her, and this audience makes her feel needed in a more extravagant, less basic way than usual.

There is so much to tell: the gardens, the courtyard, the intricate bodice of her dress. Finally, the words she chooses are the right ones; they take on the exact shape and magnificence of the moment they describe. She feels strong and alive, driving her children south on a smooth highway.

She tries not to think beyond it where somewhere there is an unfamiliar dirt road that she must find in the dark. They will arrive late, and Marie-Claude, who promised to be there for dinner, will be treated like a reckless child by Bill and Karen, who are a real family, complete with bicycles and a live-in sitter. And no matter how many games her children invent in the water or how relaxed she feels half-asleep in the sun, the sight of Bill's large, winter-tender feet hobbling down the rocky path to the beach will remind them all each day of what is gone.

"Mom," Flo says. "Where were the ghosts?"

"The ballroom was enormous and filled with these fabulous gowns and tuxes and champagne goblets. The floor was black marble, and I remember how beautiful my shoes looked against its surface. Have you ever seen black marble? It's so pure and sleek, like sapphires or the fur of a black panther."

"Is that where you saw them, on the dance floor?"

"No, I saw her in the garden." Marie-Claude feels a face, a squat forehead, the sharp edge of an aquiline nose, an ugly, distended mouth, taking shape within her. "She was young, perhaps the same age as I was then, but her face was old with sadness. She held herself straight, upright, but inside she was bent with grief."

"How did you know she was a ghost?"

"When you see a ghost, you know it. You feel it."

"Was she see-through? Did you speak to her?"

"She was different. Something about her movements. And she was so sad, the way she walked around the garden, touching petals and branches, as if she could rid some of her sadness on them. It might have been the way her mouth was shaped. I don't know. It's difficult to describe how I knew."

Flo pushes off hard from her mother's headrest and falls back in her seat. She pops a sourball out of its cellophane wrapper and, after putting it into her mouth, sighs loudly.

A sweet fake-lime smell works its way quickly to the front.

"Have I lost you?" Marie-Claude says, finding Flo's bulging cheek in the rearview mirror.

"Nothing happens in this story."

Marie-Claude has an awful impulse (because they are so rude, demanding the story she didn't want to tell, then snubbing it, Flo so impatient, Tristan already asleep) to remind them of sadness. It would be so easy to do. She waits for the resentment to subside, then continues: "She wasn't transparent, but her skin was peculiar. I'm sure that's how I knew she wasn't human."

"What do you mean, peculiar?"

"It was like patina almost, that greenish color that gets on certain metals, you know, the way that bracelet of your father's, the one he wears for his imaginary arthritis, the way that turns when he forgets to make someone polish it. That's how her skin looked up close." Instead of the woman Marie-Claude sees the wrist, its hairless skin beneath the bracelet, the puffed vein that travels from his hand to his elbow. She still loves him. If he does not come back she will never feel again what she felt touching that arm.

"I like polishing it. He doesn't make me."

"Oh, Flo, you don't remember. You used to hate it. The polish stung your eyes. Anyway, her skin was like that." Beside her, Tristan's head, which has been slipping and jerking back, slipping and jerking back, finally slides all the way over to the armrest on his door. She checks the lock and feels for a moment what he feels: that delicious surrender to sleep in the passenger seat of a car.

"I didn't hate it. And I still do it, too." Flo thinks of the chance she had to go with her father and his girlfriend, Abigail, to Manhattan instead. She had to choose between ocean or museums, a big house with other kids or adjoining hotel rooms (clicked shut at bedtime till morning). All that seems insignificant now. As always when absent, her father has become mild and soothing. She could call him, take a bus back to DC. He isn't leaving until tomorrow morning. How much could a bus ride cost?

"I did speak to her." Marie-Claude turns around to see if Flo will still listen. Flo doesn't look up from what she is doing: dropping flimsy American coins from one hand into another, then back into a pouch. "I asked her if she was enjoying the ball." Marie-Claude laughs. "I didn't know what else to ask!"

"Did you speak French or German?"

"German, I think. But she didn't reply in a voice. It was more like telepathy. But she didn't want to chat. She moved right past me, back to her old route around and around the rose garden."

"This isn't the same story."

"I've never told this story to you before, so I don't know what you were expecting."

When she told it to her husband, there were two ghosts. She had wanted him to see what they'd become. She described everything carefully, their movements, their fingers, the shapes of their mouths. *We mustn't become them, Robert, not yet.* But he didn't understand. He had stopped wanting to understand her.

"Mom, you're lying. You always do this."

"What do you mean, I always do this?"

"Change things around. Lie about the truth."

"I'm not lying, Florence." And Marie-Claude sees more clearly the scrolled, unbloomed rosebushes, the small pool, more rosebushes, and the woman traveling through. "I have never lied to you." Each time around the far edge, the woman lifts her skirt so it doesn't catch on a spigot. "I am not the liar in this family."

"Yes, you are. You lie all the time."

"Flo, I do not." For comfort, she knows she can turn to Tristan, who, still asleep, holds a comic book and her sunglasses in his lap. "Name one lie I've ever told you."

199

"You said we could take Belle with us. You promised we could."

"I thought Bill and Karen would bring their dogs, but they didn't, so I couldn't very well ask to bring ours. We're guests. It wouldn't have been right."

"But you lied. You said one thing and did another."

"Flo, that was completely out of my control. That's not a lie."

"All right, here's a better one," and this is something she's wanted to mention for a while now. "You told me that you and Daddy separated suddenly, that you were both in love all those years when I was little. You always told us that, Mom, that we were born out of love."

"That's true. It's absolutely true. We loved each other very, very much." There was no day happier in all her life than the day Tristan was born. They were living in Paris then. That morning at the market is still so vivid: the wet stalls, the bag of peaches, the young face of the vendor, the train of pimples across his neck. She was reaching over the cherries to squeeze an avocado when she felt the warmth on her legs, when she finally made the distinction between her own water and the rain. And in the afternoon, Robert brought Flo to the hospital. They climbed up on the bed with her and Tristan and pretended they didn't understand French when the nurse scolded them. That day was just a culmination of the happiness that had been pooling inside her from the moment she met Robert, yet afterward there was only more, a peaceful, languorous bliss. They had jokes about it, about how so much happiness was depressing. "All those years, Flo, right up until last year, we were happy. You were born and raised in a tremendous amount of love."

"And then something just happened, just like that?"

"I don't know." Marie-Claude can't bear to play the unknowing victim, to actually reveal how bewildered she still is. But her daughter wants the truth. "I just don't know. Whatever happened, it didn't happen to me." She looks at Flo in the rearview mirror and says softly, with no edge, "Maybe Daddy can explain it better."

"He says it happened slowly. He said it wasn't a big clap of thunder like you always say but a wave that gets bigger and bigger until it breaks."

Marie-Claude knows Flo is not making this up to hurt her; she recognizes her husband's similes, stolen from a world entirely alien to him.

"He said he'd been unhappy since before Tristan. He said he hadn't known anything about real love before he met Abigail. He says he always knows when witnesses are lying because they remind him of himself when he was—"

"Please, Flo. Please stop."

Marie-Claude slows to the speed limit. Her eyes have been on the road, but she has not been watching. All the windows in the car are open, even hers, which she doesn't remember rolling down. Warm air, much warmer than an hour ago, blows through, and she leans forward to let the wind unstick the shirt from her back. The steering wheel feels loose in her hands, unrelated to guiding the car. And the road, even at fifty-five, is disappearing far too fast beneath them.

She thinks of what she could remind her daughter of. She could tell the story of Flo's last birthday in September, which fell on a weekend she went to her father's alone, without Tristan, and how at first Flo thought he was teasing, not singing at the breakfast table, not alluding to a present hidden somewhere—behind a curtain or in the freezer—and how on the way to check the Saturday mail at his office she expected a surprise party; at lunch she waited for a cake. When he returned her on Sunday, Marie-Claude read the whole story in the raised rash on Flo's neck.

When she feels a bit more in control of the car, Marie-Claude turns to look at the outlet stores beside the highway. She wishes they were driving through France, passing cows spread flat out on a hill. In France they might come across something extraordinary, like a burning barn or a ewe giving birth. Flo might see it first and, even before she could ask, Marie-Claude would pull over. They would get out of the car noiselessly so as not to disturb Tristan and witness together the hot collapse of a building or the equally overwhelming spectacle of new life dropping onto the grass. They might squeeze each other's fingers in anticipation. But barns in France, she remembers, are made of stone.

From the slice she can see of her mother's face in the mirror, Flo knows she is mad. She decides she will just have Marie-Claude let her off at a bus station before going on to the house. There would be northbound buses every few hours. Her father will be jubilant, even more pleased than if she'd decided on New York from the start.

Her mother is not looking back anymore; Flo has caught her in too many lies. But she is not through. Before she goes, takes a bus her mother will be more than happy to put her on, she wants to catch her in another lie. "You love Tristan more than me," she says. "You do."

This is an accusation Marie-Claude has feared since Tristan was born. Until now, she never knew what she would say. Today, the answer slides out effortlessly: "He makes it easier for me, Flo. He's easier to love." She waits for a response, an opportunity to apologize or qualify, but hears only, after a long silence, the crinkling of another candy wrapper. She lets her statement linger between them, hardening into fact. It gives her strength, a sense of utter freedom. They feel like the first honest words she has ever spoken.

More than an hour later, still in the back seat, legs draped over her big duffel that she's already practiced lifting twice to make sure she can carry it to the bus, Flo remembers when she heard the story about the ghost. It was the first night she'd ever spent in her father's apartment, after the separation. Her whole life is now divided into what came before and what came after the separation. This was just after, in those first few weeks whose details are impossible to recall. But she has a flash in this hot car heading south of crying in a brand-new bed, begging her father for a story to put her to sleep. He didn't know how to tell a story, he insisted, but Flo did not believe him. *Anyone can tell a story*, she hollered at him. *Anyone.* Finally he sat on the bed and told her how when they were very young, he and Marie-Claude (and Flo remembers this, too, how he said Marie-Claude and not Maman like he used to, as if her mother were now a sister or some friend of the family) had been invited to a castle in Austria. In his version, he saw the ghosts. And Marie-Claude didn't believe him. No one did, he told Flo. They all thought he was nuts. But as the night went on, he became friends with these ghosts and, though he couldn't tell Flo exactly how, got them back to their other world safely. Remembering this ending, Flo laughs out loud.

"Look," she hears her mother say softly to herself. The ocean is suddenly beside them. They have reached the beginning of the cape earlier than expected, before dinner, before sunset. Waves crack, then flatten onshore, releasing a sour smell that quickly fills the car. Plump seabirds stand on one leg in the shimmering glaze left behind. Flo has forgotten to mention the bus station.

Marie-Claude feels Tristan stir beside her. "Look," she whispers again, and he opens his eyes onto the wide shaft of blue alongside the car, turns to her, and asks her to tell him, just once more, the one about how he was born.

THE MAN AT THE DOOR

There were two of them in the basement already, unfinished, the pages hidden in a cabinet behind the cans of paint and stain. This one was her third attempt.

Last fall she'd been on a binge, filling two notebooks on weekdays during the baby's morning nap while her husband and two older children were scattered at their own desks miles away. But now that it was winter, a familiar torpor had set in. For weeks she'd written nothing, though she couldn't break the horrid compulsion to sit there and wait.

This morning, however, without warning, a sentence rose, a strange unexpected chain of words meeting the surface in one long gorgeous arc. As she hurried to get it down, she could feel the pressure of new words, two separate sentences vying for a place next to the first, and then more ideas splitting off from each of those and where there had been, for so long now, arid vacuity there was fertile green ground and any path she chose would be the right one. Words flooded her and her hand ached to keep up with them and above it all her mind was singing *here it is here it is* and she was smiling. The baby bleated through the monitor.

She'd only managed to get three sentences on the page.

He was not the good kind of baby who cried out and then, sensing that no one was going to come running, rolled over and fell back asleep. The crying would swiftly build to a crescendo of outrage and reproach that would wipe out all hope of another sentence. She stomped up the stairs to his doorway. "What baby takes a six-and-a-half-minute nap?"

He pulled himself up, pressed his teeth into the coated crib railing, and began to sway fetchingly, grinning all the while at the cleavage within the V of her bathrobe.

"Don't you get it? I need you to sleep."

He whimpered at the ugly sounds she was making.

Her only choice was to nurse him back to sleep while she worked. She hoisted him out, squeezing him hard at his armpits. He studied her face uneasily.

She carried him to her spot at the kitchen table, latched him on, and reread the three sentences. How quickly they had flattened, lost their music. For those few words she had been rough with her son? Her eyes passed over the page again. Awful. She felt like driving the pencil through her skin. The baby sucked, his eyes shut for the long pulls and open for swallowing, unseeing the whole time. The strong tugs at her breast returned her to a more familiar self. She pressed her lips to the fuzz at his hairline and nibbled. These animal moments of motherhood obliterated everything else briefly.

Eventually he drifted off, her nipple hanging from his lips like a cigar. She read her words several more times trying not to condemn them, straining to catch the faintest echo of what she thought she'd heard before. Just as she lifted her pencil, the doorbell rang. She glanced in its direction through the walls and shook her head. It rang again. The threat of losing any more of this precious time forced another sentence out of her. Then the doorbell was held down so long the chimes played notes she didn't recognize.

"I'm not coming," she said quietly.

Sharp knocks began on the thin side window, growing louder and louder until she was certain a hand would shatter through before she could reach the door. She swung it open wide.

"That's enough!" she said in a harsh whisper. She wasn't about to wake the baby up for this man on her porch, a man who did not hesitate to knock on glass as if it were solid steel. His knuckles, she saw, were red as he dropped them into his pocket.

"What are you selling?" Usually she would have cared—about her tone, her bathrobe, the great bulb of breast and the dark brown areola still tenuously attached to the baby's mouth—but her anger consumed all weaker concerns.

He held out a thin paperback.

"No thanks," she said, more civilly now, understanding the knocking was part of a religious fervor, a feeling, perhaps accurate, that this house or half of a house (their childless neighbors were rarely home, never shared the brunt of the peddling that went on during the day) needed conversion.

"I've come from Smything and Sons," the man said.

"Who?"

"The publishing house." He shook the book at her. "They've given me this and I've come to talk to you about it."

She shifted the baby upward, hoping to cover up a little more. "Why?" She read the largest words on the cover. It was the working title of her novel, the one in the notebooks on her kitchen table. She pinched the book between her thumb and fingers but could not loosen it from the man's grasp. "Give me that." Then she let go. The sound of her own voice scared her. It was her voice as a small child. She even felt the slight resistance of the words in her mouth, as if language were still somewhat new. "Please," she added.

"That's what I've come to do. Will you have me in?"

She looked at his face for the first time. He was a familiar stranger, someone you know you haven't met but could have, perhaps should have. There was a little Bing Crosby in the heart-shaped mouth, a little Walt Whitman (when he was younger and kept his beard trimmed). There was even a bit of Gerald Ford somewhere, maybe only because she'd recently read an article about his hidden integrity and decency. It was clear that the only way she was going to discover how there could be another novel with that name, despite the searches she'd done to make sure there wasn't, was to let the man in.

So often, when she made a dubious decision like this, she followed it up extravagantly, as if flaunting it to her better judgment. She led him into their small living room and said, "Can I get you something to drink?"

"I'll take a gin martini if you've got it." He gave his trousers a quick tug before bending to sit in the middle of the couch. A diaper peeked out from beneath his left thigh though he didn't notice it. He balanced the book on his gray flannel knees. She smiled, waiting for him to acknowledge his joke. A cocktail at nine thirty in the morning.

He smiled back. "On the rocks."

"I've got coffee, seltzer, OJ, tap water."

"Hmm?"

"What can I get you, really?" Her anger was back. The baby was asleep and her writing time was dwindling. Why had she let him in?

"Here, let me help you with the martini." He nestled the paperback in the seat of the bouncy chair on the coffee table.

She followed him into the kitchen. "I'm sorry but that's not a possibility. We don't have any—"

He opened the pantry door and there, instead of the teetery plywood shelves her husband had nailed in, instead of the thin boxes of rice and couscous, instead of the baby's mixed grain cereal and jars of sweet potatoes, instead of the pasta and beans and cans of soup and the precious bottle of sun-dried tomatoes from Liguria she had splurged on but never wanted to use, was a long, glass-covered counter stocked with two chrome shakers, a strainer, a jar of onions, a jar of pimiento olives, a box of toothpicks, five glass swizzle sticks, and the ice bucket with the silver pine cone sticking up on top. She didn't have to look any farther to know that below, behind the white cabinet doors, were bottles of vodka, gin, bourbon, and vermouth or that above, upside down on paper towel lining, were her father's Class of '62 highballs, the muscular bull fading with all the trips through the dishwasher of her youth.

"I'm glad you've got Beefeater," the man said over his shoulder. "No need to get any fancier than that."

She watched the sureness of his hands, the love that went into the preparation. She had forgotten, long forgotten, the ritual of it all. She had carefully married a man who, like her, did not drink a drop.

He made his martini. She'd never noticed, as a child, the tenderness between a drinker and his drink. He didn't grab the bottle by the neck as she remembered, but lifted it with two gentle hands, one at the base and one at the belly. His hands moved delicately from ice to glass, bottle to glass, each gesture a signal of love. As a result, the liquor seemed to shine with a thousand glints and glimmers of gratitude as he carried it, close to his breast, back to his spot on the diaper on the couch. She sat down in the chair opposite him. She didn't realize until she released the weight onto the armrest what a strain the baby had been on her arms and neck. With her free hand, she reached for the book, saying, only when she had firmly secured it, "May I have a look now?"

"Of course. It's your book."

"It's not mine," she laughed. "Mine's not finished. Someone else beat me to the punch." But there was her name below the title, in a sort of swirly script she didn't like. The words ADVANCED READER'S COPY ran diagonally across the upper left corner. Was it the first of April? She was conscious of how long it took her sloggy mind to find the month. January. Even if it were April Fools', this was not in the realm of the sense of humor of anyone she knew. And no one knew about this novel.

She opened the book. On the left-hand side, opposite the title page, which again declared this to be hers, was the copyright date. She gasped.

"What is it?" the man asked between two loving, shut-eyed sips. "Two more years?"

He took in the gestalt of her life—the robe, the boob, the primary-colored plastic items on the floor, the cardboard books with corners chewed off, the bouquet of half-deflated balloons hovering in the corner—and shrugged.

She turned the page. It was dedicated to her mother. Of all people. "The jig's up now, mister." It was an odd choice of words for her, and she was reminded of walking with her mother through a parking lot, though she couldn't say why.

"I suppose you had a reconciliation."

"No chance of that. She's dead."

"But not beyond the reach of forgiveness."

She slammed the book shut, though its flimsy galley covers did not give her the effect she wanted. "Who sent you? What is this about?" She wondered if he was, after all, a religious fanatic, one of those Mormons wanting to do a little hocus-pocus on all of her ancestors.

"As I said, if you have the time, I'd like to discuss your work."

"Why should I discuss my work with you? You've never read it. No one's ever read it."

"No one?" he asked, doctorly, humoring her delusion.

"No. I keep it locked up." She'd read a part of her first novel to her husband soon after they'd met, when she could have read him cereal boxes and he'd have thought she was

213

a genius. After all his praise, she hadn't been able to write another word of it. She was careful not to read him any of the second one, but he'd stolen glances and eventually a turn of phrase had leaked out of him, something about nests of snow in the trees. He tried to placate her with compliments, threatened to publish both books himself if she wouldn't try, but she hid them in the basement, bought a box with a key, and never told him she'd begun a third.

"It would have been a waste of time for me to come here without having read your work."

"This is not my work!" Oh, why had she shouted? The baby jerked awake, shot her a pissed-off glare, and began to scream. The morning—or what was left of it—was officially ruined.

"Listen," she said above the noise, flipping madly to the first chapter. She read the first line aloud. She had approached this sentence with such resistance to ownership that the resistance momentarily outlasted the fact of her own words on the page. Then her defiance collapsed. Her baby was shrieking, and her book, half-written, locked in a box for several years, was bound in a galley in her hand.

She felt the baby's tears rolling down her stomach inside her bathrobe. She stood up and jogged him on her hip until the crying mellowed to a low, nearly satisfied hum. The man continued to sit patiently, primly, on her couch.

"Okay," she said. "What do you want to talk about?"

"I have a few suggestions, minor ones, really." He held up his drained glass. "Might I bother you for another before we begin?"

She thought about having him make it himself again, then decided she'd water it down a bit, just as she'd done to her parents' drinks before they caught on. The baby, having spied something interesting as she carried him across the room, lunged for the floor, twisting his torso out of her grip. From the kitchen she could see he'd crawled over to the sofa, pulled himself up by the piping of a cushion, and was sidestepping toward the man and the red ballpoint he'd taken from his breast pocket.

Her hands among the martini ingredients were not sure or loving. They were not even, as she half expected, the hands she'd once laid upon this bar, innocent and investigative. Her two fingers no longer fit easily in the onion jar, and the shaker, smaller too, seemed far more menacing. She felt as an atheist might, returning to the altar of her childhood. These were the tools, the chalice, cruet, and pyx, the ugly, important objects that had once worked a kind of black magic years ago.

She felt a heaviness in her limbs and spun around to tell him to go. She didn't care how the bar got here or the book with her name and her words. All she wanted was to get back to the page on her desk. But what was the point if somehow it was already finished? She had such trouble with endings. She had to get that book. She forced herself through the steps of the martini, adding a few splashes from the tap before shaking, and returned.

The man remained exactly as she had left him, though his hair (had he removed a hat?) had changed. It now seemed his most striking feature (where was Bing? where was poor, decent Gerald Ford?), a thick white covering shorn into a square with closely cropped sides and a slightly longer, iron-straight top. She was so struck by the alteration or her own lack of observation that she forgot, until after she handed him his drink, about the baby.

He was gone.

"Did you notice where Matty went?"

"Hmm?" He looked up from his notes, notes in red ink in the margins of her book.

"My little boy. He was right there."

He stared blankly back at her, as if she'd ceased speaking his language.

"Where did he go?" she said, faking calm, concealing suspicion for the moment. Was this how simple it was—a Faustian bargain—the book for the baby? The door to the stairway was shut, and he hadn't crawled into the kitchen—or had he? She raced back in, bent her head to peer beneath the table and through the pantry door. She returned to accuse. What the hell did you do with my child? She opened her mouth, then she saw him, on the fourth shelf of the bookcase, face out, feet dangling between

Hardy and Hazzard. She lunged for Matty and got him safely in her arms. Nothing in the course of this morning was as strange and impossible as the fact that her baby, her wriggling, restless, rarely sleeping, nonstopping baby, had been sitting still on a shelf for over a minute while she searched for him. In that minute, the man had downed his martini. Again she opened her mouth to scold him—you put him on the bookshelf, he could have fallen, he could have struck his head on the edge of that table!—but upon hearing her intake of breath, he glanced up, smiled the absent smile of a man absorbed, and patted the cushion beside him. "Come let's talk this over," he said.

His voice was gentle, promising great wisdom and perhaps a little necessary admonishment, with love. She went to him with sudden obedience. When he shifted his weight toward her, his clothes released the smells of the span of her life: sour apple candy, wet mimeograph ink, used paperback books, semen, baby wipes. The odor nauseated her. He held the book out but tipped away from her so she couldn't see his writing. He cleared his throat and read the first sentence. Then he looked at her with pity and struck a line though the entire first paragraph. "Now enters the father. Now it gets interesting. He is the action. She is the reaction. The action is infinitely more interesting." When she didn't immediately agree with him, he said, "Would you have preferred *David Copperfield* to have been told by Agnes?"

"Would you have preferred *Moby Dick* to have been told by the whale?"

His mouth fought with his impatience. "That falls into a different category of conflict. When it is man versus nature, then man is the action against a force. The force is not interesting in itself."

She searched frantically for a better example. "*The Great Gatsby.*"

"Oh, Scott. He barely knew how to tie his shoes in the morning let alone write a novel. Max wrote that. He wrote all those books. But let's not quibble. This book is about the father. No one will actually come out and say this nowadays, but women are at their best when they're writing about men: their husbands, their fathers, their lost loves. It's when they start writing about themselves that they become unreadable." He proceeded to cross out several more pages, shaking his head. "You simply cannot name me a book, a great book, a lasting book, that was written by a woman *about* a woman."

"*Mrs. Dalloway.*"

"Oh, now, she's the lens, not the object. She herself is the least material character in the book. That book is about the aftermath of war. It is about the rigidity, aka Richard Dalloway, the fear, aka Peter Walsh, and the insanity, aka Septimus Smith, of course, of war."

There was no arguing with this man. He could take one of her most treasured books, a book that she always felt captured her own fragile relationship with the past, a book with her favorite moment in it—Clarissa and Sally and their kiss by the stone urn—and claim that it was about war. Still, there was Jane Austen, wasn't there?

He held up his hand. "And don't talk to me about those other English women. All those books are fairy tales written by hound-faced spinsters who never got asked to dance, let alone to marry."

Her book. She needed to keep him focused on her book. "So you think it should be told strictly from the father's point of view?"

"No, no. You've entirely misunderstood me. Keep the girl, just train her eye on the father and don't let her slip into those little pity parties she has for all her *feelings*. Think"—he clenched his eyes and his jaw and his fists, then released—"Huckleberry Finn," he said. "And let's most certainly not follow her into her adulthood."

"Why not?"

"We know where she's headed. We don't have to read it. She marries, she has babies, and they fill her with love and rage. What's new or startling about that?"

He had changed again, transitioned smoothly from military to effeminate, his legs now tightly crossed, his lips in a bemused pout. His attitude reminded her of her college boyfriend, who'd passed through with his new husband last summer and sat for several hours on this same couch, watching with those same lips as she scrambled to meet the needs and whims of her three children, witness-ing over dinner a spat with her husband about a missing Hello Kitty straw. The visit had unveiled the mystery of this man's devastating ambivalence years ago, but she could have done without his but-for-the-grace-of-God relief as he hugged her goodbye.

Matty, struggling to get off her lap, scraped an unclipped fingernail across her neck and she reacted loudly, more loudly than it hurt. She put him on the ground and pointed him toward his toys, then returned her attention to her visitor, though she no longer knew what she wanted from him.

"I'll just fetch myself another." The ice, still fresh and large, rang in time with his steps. It was only ten fifteen in the morning, but she was overcome with a late-afternoon feeling from childhood, sitting at the table with a spelling book (the poem she'd written in study hall tucked safely inside) while her mother arranged fish sticks on a cookie sheet and her father carried both their glasses back to the bar. It was a perilous time of day because of its prom-ise. Her dad was singing a song about her mother's hair, which had been all poufed up that day at the hairdresser. *Is it cotton candy? Is it marshmallow? If you try and taste it, you're a brave fellow!* Her mother was laughing. If only they fed her earlier, she could leave the room now, carry away the happy little ditty, keep it separate from other words of theirs that would lodge inside her. But her mother set the timer for seventeen minutes. Her father opened a can of dog food. Then he made a joke about her mother's pocket-book, which was always in his way, always on top of the one thing he was looking for. *Like a shitting pigeon*, he said, yanking the newspaper out from under it. They kept their drinks close. Her mother slid a plate in front of her, then made her father get up from the red chair by the fridge to sit with them. He slid the spelling book toward himself and flipped to the hardest section in the back.

Okay, Sylvia. Conundrum.

Her mother was reluctant to play; she was always the first to turn sour.

You haven't even asked your daughter about her day.

C'mon, give it a shot.

All right, her mother said, taking in a deep, wary breath, *C-U-N—*

Wrong! There was far too much glee in his voice. He pointed toward the street. *Back to Cranford Junior College for you!* The windows blackened and it felt like the house was being buried alive. Her father brought two new drinks to the table. They were always so excited about a fresh drink, but all the alcohol seemed to do to either of her parents was uncover how little they liked life or anything in it. *You haven't even asked your daughter about her day.* How often her mother said that, as if it were their last hope, a white ring tossed onto the waves. She tried to say the things they liked to hear: who got A's, who got in trouble. But every night she failed. Such an uncompelling child, wholly unable, night after night, to keep her parents afloat. And then the poem slipped out of the spelling book and her mother snatched it up before she could. *What's this?* Her parents' eyes met. If they'd been wolves, they would have licked their chops.

She thought she'd disposed of these moments long ago. But now, in a house of her own, with children and a husband of her own, with dusk and dinnertime coinciding once again, they had begun to creep back in. And with them came a feeling, a presentiment, that she would eventually destroy this good life, for wasn't her need to write like her parents' need to drink? A form of escape, a way to detach? And, like the alcohol, it weakened and often angered her, left her yearning for the kind of rare and extraordinary ability she'd never have. What had her mother yearned for? She'd married at nineteen. Had one child. (*Any more would have put me in the nuthouse*, she used to say to people who asked.) Died at fifty. (Alone in a rented room, her father having left her for someone who let him be the only drunk.) After her mother's death she'd searched her drawers for clues but there was nothing but a dinner party planner and a few manila envelopes of photographs stuck together. No note, no apology (it didn't take her long to realize this was what she was really looking for). What had her mother's life consisted of? When she came home from school in the afternoons, her mother would either be on the phone or flipping through a magazine, and even though she'd be doing nothing that she couldn't continue doing now that the bus had come, a terrible wave of sadness seemed to pass through her, as if her daughter were the sun itself, setting on all her dreams. Her mother would often make herself a drink then, though she would rinse out the glass and put it back to dry on the paper towel on the shelf so that when her father came home she could pretend the one he made her was her first.

The book lay on the couch. Once again she took it in her hands. He'd crossed out nearly half the words. His red ink covered the margins of every page. He had an opinion about every choice. A grown woman would not own a toboggan! This is not the kind of man who would order a salami sandwich! She flipped again to the last chapter. It began with the four sentences she had written this morning, though he'd struck them through with triple lines, then a wavy one on top, and if she hadn't been familiar with the words already she wouldn't have been able to make them out. She'd been right; it was crap. The entire chapter was obliterated like that, his annotation no longer limited to the sides but covering the crossed-out type, the hand furious and uncontrolled, ending with a huge YOU CAN'T DO THIS!!!!! in the space left on the last page. Still, she'd had no idea she was so close to the end.

He returned. She could see the effects of the alcohol now, not in any carelessness of his movements but in their carefulness. He was in that state just before drunkenness, when the alcohol makes you more aware of your body and what it is touching. She felt that he drank for this moment: not for the dulling but rather for the heightening of his senses. There was something about the way he breathed through his nose, the way his fingertips touched the glass, the way his free hand settled in his lap as he sat back down beside her. Just watching him reminded her of the texture and temperature of things. She could feel the heat of his thigh. And yet his awareness of her had slipped a little. Her attraction to him came on fast and undeniably.

He turned to her sharply, as if she had spoken her desire aloud. He was young now, college age, with thick brown hair and those eyes, those haunted eyes that all the men who'd ever broken her heart had had. "You have more than one?" he asked.

"One what?" She could barely find a breath for the words. When was the last time her groin had throbbed so painfully?

He looked down at Matty, who had managed to put two pieces of a wooden track together for the bright-blue train to sit on. "Distraction."

"I have a million distractions," she said, hearing a long-gone flirtation in her laugh, knowing that if he touched her she would not resist. "But only three children." Usually it gave her pleasure to speak of her children—their ages, their quirks—but now they were obscuring the conversation.

"Tolstoy had thirteen children. And most of them were born while he was writing *War and Peace*. I'm not sure he even knew any of their names. That's the way it has to be done. You've got to forget your children's names."

Matty was pushing the train back and forth on the short track, making a noise she knew was "All aboard!" but to anyone else sounded like "Pla!" His long sleeves were pushed up nearly to his armpits, the way he liked them. His upper lip was tucked deep into the warm interior of the lower, which kept its slippery purchase with steady upward undulations. But when he glanced up to find her studying him, the lip was released for the sake of an enormous smile. He patted the spot on the rug beside him, mouthing *mamamamama* without diminishing the smile. He looked just like her husband then, beckoning her, eager for her. But she did not doubt Matty, did not suspect dissembling or duplicity. Why was it so much harder to believe in her husband's love for her? She thought again of the time he had quoted her line about snow like nests in the trees. They had been walking around a lake, the three of them, their oldest, Lydia, not more than four months old and tucked in the BabyBjörn inside her parka. Halfway around, he had stopped and wrapped them tightly in his arms. *My family*, he'd said, his voice a little squeak. Then, a quarter of a mile later, he said that about the snow and the trees and she marched off and he kept insisting he hadn't been mocking her. Now she could easily see he hadn't been. Of course he hadn't been. She knew now, too, that even at the time she had known he hadn't been mocking her—but she'd needed to find something to create distance, to put a wedge between her and that small squeak of joy he'd revealed to her. Monotony, especially the unfamiliar monotony of being loved, was something she couldn't seem to get comfortable with.

She slipped off the couch down to Matty, who secured her with a meaty elbow on her thigh. The man was adding more notes to the margins. He was old again, her desire for him already a ludicrous memory. "The third book is traditionally the strongest of the early works."

"This is my first."

He shot her a stern, disappointed glare. "Novels in boxes are still novels." Then he softened. "Why haven't you been able to finish them as well?"

"As well? As well as I finished this one?" He looked hurt by her disbelief in him, and she decided to try and answer him honestly. "I don't know." Matty had crawled behind her and was hoisting himself up by her hair. "That hurts Mommy," she said. "Please stop." And when he didn't, she felt the anger stir, the deep pool of it, always there. "I used to feel ambitious, I think, in college. My professors were so decent and respectful, nothing like the adults I had known before. They made me feel like I could do anything. Sometimes still, I get these burning electric jolts of, I don't know, belief, I guess. I'll write and

I'll believe. But then—" It was like those nights when she was a kid, it was just like that, her father making the jokes and her mother laughing and everything was like something to believe in and then the timer for the fish sticks goes off and we sit down and it's all shifted completely. "Then it just stops." There was a raw ache in her chest. "You have kids, and everything else becomes so . . . faint. And that old desire is like a cramp you wish would go away for good."

"But those first two books. You've done nearly all the work. Why bury them?"

"They should be burned. They're awful."

"You have trouble finding the merit in your own work."

"You do too, apparently." She pointed to the last red-splattered page.

A look of revulsion came over him, as if he'd forgotten to whom he was talking. "Well that— That last chapter is awful. It's disgusting. There's no excuse for it."

She felt a familiar weakening in her stomach muscles. She still buckled so easily under a sudden change of mood, an unexpected attack. Gone was the compassionate face, the sympathetic ear. "It is entirely unconvincing. Why do you people even try to write scenes of violence? It's not your genre; it's not in your nature." He threw the book down on the floor and stood over her. "It makes absolutely no sense." He walked to the end of the room and back. "You breach every understanding, every promise to the reader when she commits that act. Maybe someone like Bowles or Mailer could have pulled it off, but not you, honey." He shook his glass at her. "Not you."

He was one of those lightweight alcoholics, she realized. Three drinks and he was toast. Either of her parents could have six martinis and still drive her to a friend's house.

"And without a weapon. It's priceless," he cackled. "A weapon is necessary to the triad. Don't you even know that? The killer, the body, the weapon. They interact. They interchange. The Father, Son, and Holy Ghost, for Christ's sake. After a murder, the murderer is really the murdered, killed by his own lack of humanity. It's his death that is significant. The weapon stands as the judge and jury, the object that casts him out of the dream back into reality. Without it, you simply don't have murder."

She never stood up to the drunks when she was young. Not to her father or her mother, not to any of their friends on Friday and Saturday nights, their heavy hands on her hair, their strange, unchecked thoughts spoken aloud. She still remembered Mrs. Crile finding her in the TV room, stroking her, putting a hand up the back of her shirt and clucking with pity, declaring that no one ever recovers from being an only child. *Look at Richard Nixon*, she'd snorted before turning away.

"I think you're full of shit." She didn't even know what he was talking about, who could possibly die at the end of her book.

He glared at her. She was not surprised to see Nixon's small eyes and bulging jowls. "It is wrong on every level: schematically, thematically. You are meant to feel at the end of a book that what has gone on is completely unimaginable and yet inevitable. Do we feel that? No. Not to mention that no woman could bury a grown man's body in an hour. And in the backyard? In January?" He thrust out his arm toward her windows, as if this were the house of her novel. "The whole thing is an atrocity." Without asking, he headed to the kitchen for a refill.

"No," she said.

The bite in her voice jerked him like a rope. "One more, then I'll go."

"No. No more. You need to leave now."

"I'm not leaving until I get another drink," he said from the pantry, his hands having reached safety, "and you come up with a better ending."

"Get out of my house." She grabbed at his arm but only caught his coat sleeve; glass and ice shattered across the countertop.

He locked his fingers through a bottle opener fixed to the wall and she couldn't yank him out of the tiny room. With his free hand he began to make another drink. She reached behind him and shoved his arm. Another highball shattered. He took down a third and she did the same thing. He paused then, staring at all the broken shards.

"I have never understood why a person who is not a genius bothers with art. What's the point? You'll never have the satisfaction of having created something indispensable. You've got your little scenes, your pretty images, but that desperate exhilaration of blowing past all the fixed boundaries of art, of *life—that* will forever elude you." He took down another glass, waited for her to smash it, and when she didn't he quickly made his drink. His eyes wandered over her as he drank. Then he said, the liquid still glistening on his lips and tongue, "And why don't you tighten up that robe. I'm done looking at those things."

Matty was fascinated by her work, the new movements of her arms, the strange tool and its wonderful noise as she thrust it again and again into the earth, and the spray of dirt and rocks that came up over her back onto the grass, sometimes landing on the thick rubber lip of his red sneaker. He sat and watched her with more interest even than he watched the backhoes on Spring Street, digging up an old septic system. She worked hard and fast and the sweat began to mix with the milk and the tears inside her robe. She was surprised, given the season, how soft the earth was, how relenting. Soon she'd dug deep enough to step down into it. She felt its warmth curl around her ankles. Its smell was intoxicating. She'd paid so little attention to the earth in her life.

When she was done digging, she scooped Matty up and brought him into the house, fed him a small bowl of rice cereal mixed with applesauce (they were back in their regular spots on the wonderful wobbly shelves), and put him in his crib. He cried briefly, but by the time she came back downstairs and listened for him through the monitor, there was only the loud tide of his breath in sleep. She dragged the man from where he'd fallen across the pantry's narrow threshold out the back door. His feet bounced carefree down the steps. He was light and fell into the hole gracefully, like a piece of cloth, so she didn't have to get in there and rearrange him. There was no mound when she'd finished; every scoop of dirt had fit perfectly back in. She replaced the sod she'd carefully cut out and went inside. According to the clock on the stove, her work had taken forty-nine minutes.

The book was sprawled on the floor where he had flung it. She brought it over to the couch, tossed off the diaper, and lay lengthwise, on her stomach. She turned to the last chapter. The red cross-outs had faded, and it was, she could easily see now, a fine ending.

ACKNOWLEDGMENTS

I am indebted to the following people for their close reading, advice, and guidance with these stories: Don Lee at *Ploughshares*, Hannah Tinti at *One Story*, Christina Thompson at *Harvard Review*, Leigh Haber at *Oprah Daily*, Tyler Clements, Calla King-Clements, Eloise King-Clements, Josh Bodwell, Susan Conley, Sara Corbett, Anja Hanson, Caitlin Gutheil, Debra Spark, Linden Frederick, and Laura Rhoton McNeal. These pieces were transformed into a collection during a pandemic by the phenomenal people at Grove Atlantic: my brilliant and beloved editor Elisabeth Schmitz, Morgan Entrekin, Deb Seager, Judy Hottensen, Justina Batchelor, Sam Trovillion, Amy Hundley, Gretchen Mergenthaler, Julia Berner-Tobin, Paula Cooper Hughes, and Yvonne Cha. I'm deeply grateful to my dear and spectacular agent, Julie Barer. It's impossible to publish a story collection without acknowledging my high school English teacher, Tony Paulus, who taught me what a short story was, then told me to write them. A thousand thanks to my husband, Tyler, and our daughters, Eloise and Calla, for everything every day.